REVELATION
AND
RETRIBUTION

AK PITTMAN

Book design by The Book Design House

www.thebookdesignhouse.com

DEDICATION

For Bea and Steve

CONTENTS

ACKNOWLEDGMENTS

I couldn't have done any of this without my day one supporters. Of special note: Steve and Gregg, the first eyes on anything I write. My amazing editor, Jessica, never lets me off easy, always forcing me to craft a better story. To my original day ones, AP and J4, you know how I feel.

PART I:
1

Juicy was a filthy man. Not in a "I just spent four days hiking through the Appalachians, and the closest thing I've had to a shower was the dip in the creek" kind of way, but in the "I've spent the last four years of my life on the street, sleeping in alleys, eating thrown-out leftovers, drinking tall boy Budweisers— or on a good day a bottle of Canadian LTD Scotch whiskey (known as 'last two dollar'), and defecating in abandoned buildings preferably but anywhere semi-private realistically, though I'm not overly concerned with making sure none of the shit is stuck to my leg" kind of way.

Juicy hadn't always been a filthy man. He hadn't always called the 'row his home. He was once Robert Harris: high school and trade school graduate; mechanic by day, bowling and dart league superstar by night; divorced yet devoted father of two boys, owner of a two-bedroom bungalow and nice pre-owned sedan, with many of his free hours spent in the backyard with Lulu.

Not quite Camelot, but a shining example of the American dream nonetheless.

When Robert smoked his first rock of crack cocaine, he knew he would only do it that one time. When he lost his job, he knew he'd get another one. When his ex-wife stopped letting Tony and Robert Jr. come around, he knew he'd make it up to them. When he lost the house, his remaining family and friends, and the last of his savings, he knew he'd always have Lulu. Lulu was his baby. Lulu was the love of his life.

Then Lulu was gone.

And when Robert, his transformation into Juicy nearly complete, had watched Lulu's custom taillights disappear into the night, he knew that in her now vomit-stained, slept-in, pipe-burnt leather driver's seat, his benefactor sat, smug in his superiority. Juicy had let the bubbling indignation pass and instead thumbed the seven hundred dollars he'd been paid for Robert's 1967 jet black, fully restored Chevrolet Impala: Lulu.

The weekend Juicy had planned with his proceeds would be glorious. He would rent a room on the 'row—one of those hourly rate, "would be condemned if anyone of consequence ever cared" rooms. He'd get some Jack Daniel's Black Label whiskey to drink, because Lulu had filled his pockets, and this weekend wasn't one for LTD. He'd get a whore for company—a sexy one who would laugh at his jokes, make him feel important, *and* satiate his every carnal need. Most importantly, he'd get some rock. None of that stepped-on, 80-20 baking soda shit for Juicy. This weekend was all about that *snap*—the good shit, the real shit, the—get-you-so-high-God-Himself-has-to-look-up-to-see-you—type shit.

A short time later, Juicy was in his nirvana. As he laid bareback against the headboard, a blonde named Sandy—who in a former life had been Emily, who might pass for eighteen but wasn't—bobbed between his legs. His eyes closed, lighter in one hand, straight pipe to his lips—he struck it and let the flame take him higher.

That snap made the telltale cracking sound, and the long, clear, slender tube was instantly milky white. He didn't stop sucking until his lungs were full, and he let the smoke stay there. He stripped every ounce of over-God high from it before exhaling in a mouth-numbing stream.

While Juicy was in a state of euphoric, crack-cocaine-induced sexual bliss, Sandy—the former Emily who might've passed for eighteen but wasn't, past high school cheerleader and honor roll student—was working. Not in the way Juicy had thought, but in the way he would've expected had he not been an infant on the 'row.

When the door broke from its hinges, Juicy's first real lesson in the street began.

"A'ight nigga, 'bout dat time."

Juicy flinched, about to defend himself and, most importantly, his stash.

"Aw nah, son. My nigga, dis nigga need some act right," the man said to two others who appeared through the open door.

"Crack-head-ass nigga on some dumb shit," one of the other thugs agreed.

Juicy was a fast learner, and he'd seen the scene in panoramic clarity: the sudden pinch of teeth in the most sensitive area; the pistol pointed at him, seemingly bigger than the man who held it; the two men who now stood over him; and the realization that his weekend of Lulu's proceeds was concluded in twenty-five minutes, an unfinished blowjob, and one long, glorious pull into that snap.

Sandy and her crew had taken everything: the rock, the cash, the drink, the smokes, even Juicy's clothes, and for good measure, they beat him unconscious with the pistol.

Four years later and Juicy had never again come close to the promise of that weekend. His days and nights consisted of getting money—by *any* means— and going to buy some stepped-on, 80-20 baking soda shit. Rinse and repeat. It was pathetic, even by Juicy's standards.

So when the offer came from the stranger he'd never seen before—a proposal no one who wasn't a desperate, repugnant soul like Juicy would even listen to—he saw a golden beacon of salvation, steeped in that good shit, whores, and drink.

In service of that offer, Juicy now ran—or fast-limped because his right ankle was disfigured courtesy of the 'row—hounded by men who would kill him if they caught up. Despite his injury, Juicy easily kept in front of his pursuers. And even as they gave chase, the dealers knew it was probably fruitless. One truism on the 'row: you can't catch a crack-head. The four men chasing Juicy were motivated by money, by revenge. Juicy was motivated by the rock, the sweet, cloying goodness of that snap. The snap won the race more times than not.

Juicy scaled the fence of the junkyard and fell ten feet to the ground. He kept moving, unconcerned with the nerve endings that ignited his wretched body in pain and the new gashes that painted his arms and legs red.

Other than a single light post in the center of the junkyard, the expansive mounds of discarded vehicles and construction equipment were shrouded in darkness. Outside a rather measly ring of light, every inch of the yard screamed *perfect hiding spot.* Slip into here and wait out your pursuers, and when they give up, make sweet love to that snap.

Tonight, Juicy inexplicably headed right for the light post. And he headed there against his better judgment, because that's where the stranger had told him to go.

Under the light post, gripping the rock with both hands, Juicy watched the four men approach, sweating with anger and exertion in the cold night. He heard their curses and threats, but his eyes searched only for the stranger.

Muthafucka said he'd be here. Don't do me like this. Don't do me dirty.

Juicy continued to probe the night until he was surrounded. His benefactor, the stranger with a promise only a crack-head as desperate and pathetic as Juicy would believe, had abandoned him.

He fingered the rock and started to beg. The dealer he'd punched a short time ago when he'd snatched the rock because of the promise, returned the favor. Juicy was greeted by four pairs of feet the instant his body hit the ground. With the merciless delight of children stomping upon ants, the feet pummeled him. He could feel his bones breaking under the torrent. Blood poured from his mouth and all those gashes, the ones he'd been so indifferent to, until he couldn't tell if more of his blood was *on* him or *in* him.

Juicy was just about to call it quits when the first of the feet stopped kicking and the man attached to them fell to the ground beside him, with less of a head than one would consider functional. Another quickly followed, just as headless. The remaining two took very different approaches to the situation that now befell them.

One ran into the shadows, shooting blindly, his pistol cocked to the side just the way the movies had shown him. Full of bluster and bravado, he was hell-bent on finding the one responsible. He dived into the vast field of twisted metal and debris. His search was not in vain. The void swallowed his curses and bluster in a single report.

The last one, the smart one in Juicy's estimation, ran the other way, away from the dark abyss that had stolen his friends' heads. But his reward was no less immediate, his death no less final.

Four perfect shots, four perfectly still bodies. Juicy, with blood seeping from wounds too numerous to count and bones too mangled for repair, managed to smile wide. He licked chapped lips, the numb taste of promise already dancing over his tongue. Never mind that he couldn't walk on his busted nubs, he would manage. At the sound of shoes on broken glass, bits of metal and dirt crunching under a slow gait, Juicy almost wept.

Fifteen hundred mufuckin' dollas.

That was the price of his beating and the heads of four drug dealers. Well worth the cost.

They shit was doo doo anyway.

He'd go downtown to Wash Ave., where all the rich white kids went, and get that good shit.

The stranger, clad in black, finally stood above him, and extended his arm down toward Juicy. Juicy reached his disfigured arm upward and grasped the gloved hand with gnarled, calloused fingers. He could almost feel Sandy's head bobbing.

Imma get that bitch. Imma fuck that bitch. Imma beat that bitch's ass. I might even kill that bitch.

His mind so enthralled with the prospect of reliving his first weekend on the 'row the *right* way, Juicy only slightly registered that he'd been turned around, and the man now gripped his throat from behind. The blade entered the left side of his abdomen. He struggled weakly against the stranger's grip. The scream he knew should be echoing through the darkened junkyard died in the viselike hold. Feeble smacks on the man's arm were the extent of his defense.

The man's lips were so close that Juicy felt his hot breath on his ear. Rhythmic breaths. Calm breaths.

"Wicked," the man whispered.

In no hurry, the man guided the blade in an agonizingly slow arc across Juicy's stomach. In a former life, Robert Harris would've known that a version of *seppuku*, ritual Japanese disembowelment of a dishonored samurai, had befallen him.

In this life, Juicy the crack-head died smelling of his own shit, keenly aware of his predicament, but still wondering if the stranger was going to give him his *fifteen hundred mufuckin' dollas*.

2

A haze of cigarette smoke already hovered near the ceiling when the alarm clock sprang to life. Classic rock blared from the tiny speakers, shattering the tranquil quiet with high-pitched wails and clamorous instruments.

The man lying prostrate in the bed was still, content to let AC/DC play out their highway song—his favorite—while he finished the cigarette.

Eventually, or *finally* to neighbors rudely serenaded by Angus Young's ear-splitting guitar riffs, Detective Pat McConnell reached over and turned down the volume.

His cell phone vibrated on the night table. He picked it up with his right hand while his left absentmindedly caressed the pillows next to where he'd slept. A millisecond after muscle memory betrayed him, Pat snatched his hand back to his chest, wringing his fingers disdainfully. He growled.

"You all right there, chief?" the caller asked.

Pat glared at the empty bed an instant longer.

"Hey, Lou," he responded. "What's up?"

"Nada, Kemosabe. Just a few DOAs done in a most heinous fashion."

Pat glanced at the clock. 5:55 a.m. Even after eight years, he couldn't get used to his partner's morning disposition. Too happy. Too awake.

"Be down in five," Pat said.

Twenty minutes later, Detective McConnell emerged from the ground floor of his downtown loft apartment building. Inside the idling Crown Victoria, Detective Lou Maguire sat behind the wheel, juggling a steaming cup of coffee and his third or fifth Old Town glazed donut.

Pat got in on the passenger side without a word of salutation, and Lou didn't expect one. Lou could tell anyone, and had, precisely how their morning would begin: Pat would be wearing dark trousers, a matching tie, and a white button-down shirt—never a jacket, hat, or gloves, no matter what the temperature. Within a minute of pulling away from the curb, Pat would inevitably rub his beard, which, like his hair, was dark brown, spotted with flecks of silver. He would sigh, looking out the window, light a cigarette, and grab for the waiting cup of coffee. Then their day could get started.

"What's the story?" Pat asked.

Lou scarfed down the last of his breakfast and discarded the empty half-dozen donut box.

"All I know is we got five DOAs at a junkyard up on Broadway. Past that, Kemosabe, I got zilch."

Pat scrunched his eyes together. Five DOAs was a

bit unusual, a bit much. St. Louis' presence on the list of most dangerous cities was well earned, but even so, five dead at one scene was atypical.

Ten minutes later, the two detectives pulled up at the junkyard. They parked on the street and walked toward the opened gate. Pat, as usual, took the lead. A small crowd of miscreants, day laborers, nosy onlookers, and a few reporters had already amassed at the police tape.

Pat didn't like the media, but at least they had some pretense for being there. The "gaggle of fools" on the other hand, held a special place of contempt in his heart. Pat hated whatever it was inside a human being that made the most vile also the most fascinating. More blood, more guts, more interest. He pushed through the gathered people with more vigor than necessary and greeted the uniform at the police tape.

"Morning, detectives," Patrolman Riggs said as he led them to the first body, just inside the fence line. "This here is vic number one. Single shot to the back of what's left of his head. We have three more in close proximity to each other just behind the trailer, and farther back is our last one."

The detectives stepped closer to the body. Pat kneeled and lifted the black, police-issued tarp. Lou whistled, long and low.

Pat rubbed his beard and examined the body. White tennis shoes, black jeans, white T-shirt, brown jacket, chain, fake solitaire earrings, Glock 9mm stuffed inside pants, pockets filled with cash of random numerations: drug dealer. He pulled out a pen flashlight and checked the entry wound. No powder burns. The shooter had been at least a few feet away.

"All right, Riggs, lead the way."

Riggs took the detectives deeper into the yard, around the back of a trailer that doubled as an office, and over to a raggedy light post. Along the way he gave them the vitals: called in at 4:30 a.m. by the junkyard owner. He'd arrived and secured the scene, no perps or witnesses.

"And," Riggs exclaimed as they reached the light post, "These are two, three, and four."

Riggs used one hand to remove the tarp and the other to cover his nose with a handkerchief.

"Well, this is different," Lou noted.

Pat kneeled over the bodies, inspecting the two men with bullet holes quickly. Except for the slight differences in entry wound location, they mirrored their compatriot. The killer had spent more time with the third man here.

"He's number five," Pat said. "He was alive when the others were done. He was killed slow and personal."

"Somebody beat the crap outta him first," Lou replied.

Pat grunted in agreement and walked toward the back of the yard. Lou and a confused Riggs watched him disappear behind a pile of lumber. For several minutes the pair stood in silence, Riggs nervous and on the verge of losing his breakfast, Lou completely at ease.

"Anything, anyone been moved?" a voiced yelled down to them.

Riggs looked around, searching for Pat's location.

"Not by us or the owner," Riggs answered, facing the wrong direction.

A few minutes later Pat reappeared with oil smudges on his arms.

"Head out front and put names to the four horsemen here. And tell the lab guys to get back here now."

Riggs left hastily without replacing the tarp, leaving the two detectives next to the gory scene.

"Well?" Lou asked.

Pat replaced the tarp and said, "The shooter was up on that pile. Vic back there was shot from above and in the face."

He sighed hard and rubbed his hands across his eyes.

"Goddammit, this doesn't make any sense. We got a junkie who got on the bad side of the four jackasses here. They're beating his ass, right?"

"Yep," Lou answered.

"But then they stop. Why? 'Cause somebody with a big fucking gun made 'em stop. So we got one and two here; they get done first. Don't even pull their weapons. Bam, bam. Then we got the other two. Mr. Tough Guy sees his boys get popped, so he goes back there. He's gonna handle it. Bam, one to the face. And we got Mr. Speedy out front. He sees all his boys get dead: one, two, three. Oh, he's shitting his pants. He's gonna beat it the hell outta here. Bam, right through the back of the head. And meanwhile, our little guy here is still alive, in the middle of all this shit. Then, to top it all off, he gets gutted. Make sense to you, Lou?"

Lou's response was muted by the arrival of the lab techs, which Pat quickly pointed toward the shooter's spot.

"Not a bit," Lou answered when they were alone again.

"Let's go find the somebody who didn't hear no evil, see no evil."

The pair returned to the entrance of the junkyard. From there Lou continued to the cruiser while Pat watched as Riggs made his way through the now-dissipating crowd, asking the usual battery of questions. They'd performed that particular dance hundreds of times before. Guy gets killed in the middle of downtown, for whatever reason, by whatever means, and there's no shortage of upstanding people clamoring to tell the police what they did or didn't see. Down on the 'row, where no one ever wants to be caught talking to the law, things work a bit differently. When the time comes, they scatter like flies. The trick is picking the right fly.

The exodus had already begun. The fast walkers and the slow strollers, scratch them both. Fast walkers: people who don't want to talk for their *own* reasons. Strollers: people who have their own reasons but want you to know they aren't scared of you.

Just to the left of the crowd, Pat thought he'd found who he was looking for: a woman, old in experience but young in years, her face gaunt, her head down, with wide eyes fixed directly on her fast-moving feet, arms crossed over her chest. Her body language was a neon sign: don't look at me.

Once she'd made it an appropriate distance from the scene, she looked behind her. She met the eyes of the detective. She held his gaze an instant too long and, more damning, ended it an instant too soon. She glanced to his right at a pile of rusted car parts, then behind her, and then everywhere else she could think of to seem uninterested before looking back down to her *faster*-moving feet.

Cookie jar, kid. Gotcha.

While she played hot potato, Pat turned to signal Lou, who was already pulling the cruiser around to follow. Of the few dozen people milling in and around the junkyard that morning, only two registered the sound. And only one of them cared. A tow truck's horn blared repeatedly at jaywalkers. Pat's eyes shot back to the woman. Her feet still carried her away, but her eyes now locked on the inauspicious sight of a police cruiser pulling into the street.

Don't do it. Don't do it. He begged silently. *Goddammit!*

She ran.

3

Richard Charles was a slave to ritual. He was up early, as usual. He jumped out of bed and right onto the treadmill for interval cardio, the first of his two workouts, heavy weights to come later in the day.

An hour later, he'd showered and shaved, his chiseled body misted with a light layer of Clive Christian cologne, hair perfectly gelled with no hint of product, white strips on and then off his teeth. After two shakes—one protein the other a variety of greens, a tooth scrub, and the draping of his body into a tailored Gucci suit, Richard drove his S Class Mercedes out of the gated community where he lived.

A short time later he pulled up at the first of his stops: Maximum Pleasure Massage. The converted two-family dwelling was home and work to some of the best sex workers in the Midwest. The door buzzed as Richard approached. He walked in through the lobby, pausing to smirk at two johns on the couches, trying their damnedest to be invisible behind magazines. He went through a second door and down a dimly lit corridor, past sealed rooms emanating sounds of Oscar-worthy acting, to the room at the end.

Inside the tiny office, a bespectacled man wearing a dark double-breasted suit sat behind a neat desk concentrating on a crossword puzzle. Occasionally his eyes would float over the wall of monitors that displayed the women plying their trade. It wasn't voyeuristic yearning that brought his eyes to the peep show, just a job.

"Mr. Charles," the man said in greeting.

Richard nodded. He needn't waste his time speaking to underlings. The briefcase he'd come for was on the floor next to the desk. He grabbed it and turned on his heel, the words "Good day, Mr. Charles" following him out.

Shortly thereafter, Richard pulled into a gravel parking lot on the south side of St. Louis. Through tinted windows, he gazed at the dump he was about to enter with unabashed scorn. Wearing a slightly less-pronounced scowl, he got out and started across the parking lot, leaving the key in the ignition.

Richard found great irony in the gesture. In his home neighborhood, the affluent St. Louis suburb of Chesterfield, he would never leave the keys inside his car. Down here where he was known—or more significantly, his employers were known—he never gave it a second thought.

A few grungy, thick-bearded, heavily tattooed men stood on the bar's porch, tipping back cans of Milwaukee's Best. Their proficiency was stunning. In the time it took him to cross the parking lot, they each opened and drained two cans. The empties joined what looked to be several cases of discarded aluminum at their feet. Richard was never quite sure if this was an early morning or late night for them. Either way, it disgusted him.

They greeted him with sidelong glances and belches. He passed them without a word. Inside, he headed directly for the bar. A man equally filthy and tattooed, though not quite as bearded, waited for him with nervous eyes.

"Morning, Mr. Charles," the man stammered.

Richard rolled his eyes, irritation building at the excuse he could see coming.

"So sorry, sir, delivery ain't here yet. Mo just called, right before you walked in. Said he'd be here in five minutes."

Richard sighed and looked at his Rolex. "Five minutes."

He meant it as a threat, and the bartender took it as such.

"Y-y-yessir. Five minutes. Swear to God. Can I get you a drink? Anything you want. On the house."

Richard pulled out a stool and took a seat. He didn't dignify the man's stupid offer. Not a thing in this dump would ever touch his lips. Frequenting the lower rungs like Maximum Pleasure and the shit hole he was now forced to wait in was not among the highlights of his otherwise glorious life, but it did pay the bills.

"The Mafia isn't dead," he'd once said to his lawyer.

"We've diversified, adapted, gone corporate. Delegation is the key. Let the niggers and spics take the headlines. Better for us. As long as our percentages keep coming, they can do as they please. They get caught. Who cares? There's always another spook."

A portion of those percentages was now five minutes late, albeit due from what he'd consider white trash, but late nonetheless.

Sitting on the teetering, second-hand stool, ears assaulted by some southern rock band, Richard realized he'd never been inside Land's End Bar & Lounge for this length of time before. He now bathed in low-class ambiance. The aromas of cheap beer, stale cigarette smoke, and body odor mingled and climbed into his nasal passages, taking up residence like the world's most revolting squatter. His eight-hundred-dollar-a-bottle cologne never stood a chance.

The visual was no better. A layer of dust covered virtually every distressed stool and broken-down, splintered table. Any reflective surface was adorned with a layer of grime. Richard stood and pulled his blazer more tightly around his body. He looked at his watch.

How long does five minutes take?

He sighed and canted his head upward. In that instant, he decided this would be the last time he stepped inside the commode known as Land's End Bar & Lounge. Above his head, hanging from every conceivable appendage—rafters, ceiling fans, and vents—were bras and panties, the sheer size of some of them and the nothingness of others equally astounding. Richard fought down an upward surge of protein shake while contemplating the *actual* source of the body odor around him when he heard tires skid to a stop on the gravel parking lot.

Thank God!

The sound of heavy boots thudded across the porch and then stopped, the pause accentuated by loud, gregarious salutation and conversation. Richard shot a death stare at the bartender.

"Mo, get your fat ass in here," he yelled.

The exchange on the porch continued unabated. The bartender's eyes bucked, veins danced across his forehead, rabid spittle settled at the corners of his mouth.

"Moooooo! Get your fat ass in here. *Now!*"

The tone on the porch became acquiescent, and a moment later a giant man wearing jeans, boots, and, judging by its worn appearance, an original Guns-N-Roses tour T-shirt appeared. The gap-toothed smile plastered on his face and remnants of Milwaukee's Best on his beard and overgrown belly infuriated Richard. He glared hard in the smiling giant's direction.

Those who don't understand that this is a business have no place in the business. Be late, fine, but damn sure be sorry.

The jovial idiot before him should at the very least have been downtrodden, and preferably on his knees begging. Richard decided right then that Mo would soon be a dead man.

The fat man took a step into the doorway, and Richard became a prophet. The top half of Mo's head disappeared, though oddly he continued to wear that gap-toothed smile. Bloody brain matter and bits of skull showered the filthy area around him.

Richard and the bartender passed each other in midair over the bar. The bartender ran toward the door, while Richard, now prone on the floor, thumbed his cell phone and retrieved his .45 from its holster.

Gunfire erupted on the porch. The drunken twins outside were returning fire. By the time the bartender made it to Mo's dead body, now wedged in the door, the porch had quieted.

The bartender grabbed Mo under the arms, dug his boots in, and pulled. He groaned under the strain of three hundred pounds of dead weight, but his great effort was for naught as a white-hot bullet cratered the crown of his head.

Thirty seconds of clamor and four dead men later, it was now church-quiet inside the bar, aside from the southern rock still coming from the ancient jukebox.

But this was of no real concern to Richard. He had made the call as his employers requested. There was nothing else to do but retrieve the briefcase and get out of here. Or die trying. His employers liked him. If he came back without their percentage, they'd like him a lot less. No money equaled his complicity in its disappearance. He'd be as dead as the smiling idiot.

Through a coating of slime that smelled faintly of ammonia, he crab-walked along the floor behind the bar and hazarded a glance around the edge. He listened for the sounds of assault for just an instant before he was up. He stayed low as he traversed the distance to the dead men and, more significantly, the briefcase. Richard peeled the giant's fat fingers from the handle and held the briefcase to his chest.

He was breathing hard. Sweat and floor slime had smeared together over his hair and clothes. Richard closed his eyes and took several mind-clearing deep breaths.

His eyes burst open, and he was gone. He hopped over Mo and the bartender and leapt the porch railing with the skill of an athlete. Mornings of interval cardio, nights of squats and deadlifts propelled the man across the gravel lot at blinding speed. Head low, briefcase up, he zigzagged around a few cars until he was soaring across the hood of his S Class.

He could hear sirens in the near distance, but they were of no consequence. Richard snatched open the door of the luxury sedan and dove inside, tossing his gun and briefcase onto the passenger seat. He stayed low as he threw the car into drive and punched the gas.

Then he was on the avenue, and Land's End was in the rearview, no pursuit in sight. In the safety of his car, with two successful pickups in hand, Richard's thoughts turned to vengeance. His fingers shook in fury as he dialed his contact.

"Yeah, I got out."

He pulled over at a stop sign and angrily slammed the car into park. He checked his rearview while his colleague on the other end of the phone asked the usual questions.

"How the hell should I know?" he screamed. "Probably somebody those tweaker assholes scammed. I tell you what, though, the stupid cocksuckers should've waited five more minutes. Cocksuckers think they can hit Richard Charles? Get on the street, talk to every cop on our roll, get me a name. That cocksucker, his family, his dog, I'm killing every one of them."

Another question from the phone sent Richard into a new litany of profanities and threats on his assailant's distant family members. He glanced in the rearview. Where the reflection of the avenue should have been, there was only blackness.

"What the—" Richard started.

The rest of his words were muffled by repeated collisions of his face with the walnut steering wheel. Richard reached for the passenger seat. His middle finger had just touched the cool metal handle of the .45 when a pain more intense, more acute than he'd ever felt radiated through his body.

The mutilation of his hand offered no pause in the assault on his head and face. The collisions continued with cartoonish ferocity and speed.

He hit the gas. The S Class engine revved hard, but the car didn't move. He held down the accelerator until the beating left his foot slack.

The attack culminated in a final skull-cracking meet with the finely crafted steering wheel. Then Richard's head was wrenched backward so violently some of his hair was yanked from the root. Blood from his broken face flowed down his throat.

He could feel breath on his ear. He knew someone was speaking, but with the pounding inside his head, he couldn't understand what he was hearing. Scorn? Mourn?

Whatever. I couldn't care less.

He tried to respond with something defiant like, *you just signed your own death warrant,* but he didn't have the strength to talk.

The man in the backseat leaned over Richard. He grabbed the seatbelt and wrapped it around Richard's neck. Richard pulled at it with his good hand, trying to loosen the noose as if it were a tie. Then the man reached to Richard's left. The driver's door opened and quickly shut again. The battered man attempted to spit blood on his attacker, succeeding only in putting a giant glob on his own shirt.

The man ripped the blade from what remained of Richard's right hand. It registered a feeling that vaguely resembled pain, but felt a million miles away, like someone else's body.

Good.

He managed to smile, cocky—his last act of defiance while he waited for the end to take him. In the seconds that followed, Richard steeled himself. No blow came. No shot, no blade. He moved his head, tightening the wrapped seat belt, and stared into the rearview. The backseat was empty. If his face wasn't so disfigured and swollen, Richard Charles would have laughed.

Stupid cocksucker. I ain't dead. You came at Richard Charles and didn't finish the job. I'm gonna make you pay.

Richard, tied up and beaten, with one mangled hand and a face that would make roadkill feel pity, was emboldened. His mind moved swiftly to the revenge he would exact on the man so stupid as to come at Richard Charles.

He needed to open the door. He'd suffocate before anyone checked on the Mercedes with limo tint because no one messed with Richard Charles's car down here.

He reached for the door. When his hand found no handle, Richard was puzzled. When the pain made it through the flood of endorphins his brain had released, the questions ceased. The panic commenced.

Richard found new strength as he tore at the seatbelt wrapped around his neck. He bucked and kicked, ever tightening the noose. He slammed his elbow into the window until the bone splintered. When he'd made both of his arms useless, he resorted to using his head.

As the flames made their way through the thick driver's seat and onto his pants and blazer, Richard Charles's last conscious act was one of belated understanding.

Burn. *The sick cocksucker had said burn,* he thought a moment before he was engulfed in fire.

4

"What a day," Lou said.

The rotund detective sat at Pat's kitchen table, rubbing his head. Pat stood in front of the refrigerator with both doors open. His eyes floated over the choices: Bud Light for garden-variety days, rum for bad ones, or... He reached into the freezer, *for worse days*, grabbed a bottle, and went to the table with two glasses.

"Yeah, real fuck of a day," Pat agreed, filling the tumblers with Jägermeister.

Pat drained the thick, tangy liquor in a single gulp. Lou demurred. Pat drank it for him and refilled his own glass. Lou looked around him into the cavernous loft. It was almost completely bereft of furniture.

"You okay there, Kemosabe?"

Pat glared across the table.

"All right, all right, you're fine. Put the daggers away, will ya?"

"How about we concentrate on today—that good with you? You remember the dead guys, right?"

Lou shook his head and flipped open the thick case

file. He spread glossies from the two crime scenes across the table. Pat stood over them and stared through a growing haze of cigarette smoke.

"What's the connection?"

"They're all dead. Especially those two," Lou remarked. He glanced down at his notebook. "Richard Charles, well-to-do mafia bagman, and Robert Harris, aka Juicy, homeless addict. They both got healthy jackets: extortion, armed criminal action, assault, solicitation, B and E, possession, possession with intent. Yeah, a coupla real *saints*. But connected? Nah, the odd couple they ain't."

Not a fucking chance, Pat thought. "Agreed. So why are they done so different? Why not just ventilate them like the others?"

"Privacy. He hated them more. Hell, maybe just to make a point," Lou replied.

"And that would be?" Pat asked.

"You got me."

They were silent for a time. Pat paced and smoked. Lou buried his face in the case file. The big detective suddenly leaned back in his chair and let loose a howling cackle. Pat shot an incredulous glare his way.

"Buddy boy, you shoulda seen it. That girl left you in the dust."

Pat wanted to be mad, but one look at the grass and oil stains that decorated his slacks after his failed attempt at catching the witness had a smile tugging at his lips.

"And I suppose you're suggesting you would've

caught her?"

"Hell no, she woulda beat my fat butt too. But I had the good sense to drive after her," Lou replied with a wink.

"Uh-huh." Pat exhaled in a long stream as he looked at the photographs again. "We're looking at this the wrong way."

"How you figure?" Lou asked, still grinning.

"We got ten dead, not two. What's it matter how they were done? Chopped, crispy, or shot—just as dead. What's the why? That's the connection."

"I don't know about that, chief," Lou said. "Look at the planning that went into it. Five and five, two different sides of town, one of 'em done in broad daylight, and all we got is a girl half-crazed on dope who thinks she saw the recently deceased Mr. Harris near a car that mighta been blue or mighta been green. He, supposing it's a he, took the time to do that to two of them. That's gotta matter."

Pat didn't agree, but his retort was cut short by a buzzing on his hip.

"McConnell," he answered.

He paused for a minute and bowed his head. He breathed a heavy sigh and closed the phone. Pat pinched the bridge of his nose and leaned back, dejected.

Lou shook his head, unbelieving. "You gotta be freaking kidding me."

Pat turned to the sink, splashed water on his face, and retightened his tie.

"How many?" Lou asked as he stood to put his blazer back on.

"Five more. A serial. Lou, we got a fucking serial."

5

Father Walter Brown sat inside the confessional reading the Holy Bible, specifically the gospel according to Luke on this night. His recollection of the New Testament near flawless, the priest did not read for study but to feed his soul. Every night he was there, with his grandmother's worn King James Bible on his lap—a family heirloom dear to his heart—and the shadow of a candle flame dancing across the pages.

Father Brown preferred the time in the confessional be spent as it was intended: men and women coming to him to cleanse themselves of sins they'd committed—or better, sins they had *yet* to commit.

At this, the witching hour, the hour of sin, what sense does it make to close the door to salvation?

The sudden sound of footfalls echoing down the corridor stirred him. He turned his head and closed the Bible as the door to the confessional slid open.

"How long has it been since your last confession?" he asked.

"Father, I don't come to you for absolution."

"My son..."

"My sin is as a child of man, and there is no absolution for being born."

"I think our Lord and Savior would disagree with that particular sentiment."

The man sighed. "Maybe you're right. When my work is done, God willing, perhaps you and I will discuss the validity of your point."

Father Brown smiled into the screened wall. He knew that, in general, comfort comes before confession. To be naked, even behind a veil, takes a certain amount of trust. God sees all, knows all, *and forgives* all. Expecting His representative to hear your most salacious tales without judgment is an entirely different matter.

"Tell me, what is it that troubles you, my son?"

"I am not troubled, Father, but burdened."

There was a rhythm to this dance. Father Brown was accustomed to it. "What is it, then, that burdens you?"

"My work. Father, I killed fifteen people. Today."

The man then recounted, in vivid detail, the murders he'd committed. There was no deceit or joy in his voice, only the quiet assurance that comes with steadfast conviction. He believed himself to be firmly in the right.

Father Brown turned toward the screened wall. He stared at it for a long time. He was confident the confessor on the other side was doing the same.

The small compartment felt suddenly cramped, the air heavy and hard to breathe. Father Brown pulled at the collar of his cassock. He wiped away the beads of sweat that now dotted his forehead. An unfamiliar emotion—rage, coupled with unbridled revulsion—burned inside the holy man. He struggled to bury the feelings, to remember he was one who believed all things, *all* men could be redeemed through Christ.

"My son, you can find forgiveness in the Lord, but you must stop what you're doing. You must repent. Atone for your actions."

It sounded weak even as he uttered it.

"Tomorrow I will kill more. And the day after, and the day after that, until my work is done. I do desire forgiveness," the man said, resigned. "But not for my work. The ones I kill, the wicked, reap only what they've sown."

The *priest* was losing his battle with the *man.* He raged.

"And you, are you pleasing in our Lord's sight? What is it that makes you righteous?"

Hearty laughter from the other side surprised, then further enraged, the priest.

"Father, do you still bring your grandmother's Bible to the confessional?"

"Of course I do," he snapped, failing to acknowledge the red flag that question should have raised.

"Tell me, then, do the words of Christ, 'You unbelieving and perverse generation', still not ring true today? Do they?"

"Hypocrite," Father Brown answered, seething. "From within, not without, proceed evil thoughts, adulteries, fornications, and murders, which defile the man. You dishonor the words of Christ with *your* perverse actions."

Father Brown could feel the man stand. He did as well. They were no longer confessor and priest but two combatants, each armed with their own moral authority.

"Still then there are the words of Paul, who said knowing the judgment of God, that they which commit such things are worthy of death. Not understanding. Not forgiveness. Death, Father. Death."

"And you! 'For wherein thou judgest another, thou condemnest thyself; for thou that judgest doest the same things.' There is no righteousness here. Hubris, perhaps. Madness, assuredly. But no, you are no more fit to judge—"

"If not me, then who?" the man yelled. "Or shall we continue to watch while the wicked beget wickedness and trample the meek?"

The shouts—one of validation, the other of recrimination—filled the empty church until the man sighed, his anger abated.

"Father, I don't require your approval, only your acceptance, and if not that, then nothing. I will destroy the wicked so the righteous may prosper. If by staining my hands with the blood of evil men I consign my soul to share their fate...so be it."

Father Brown heard the steps fade even as he remained standing, hands clenched, eyes boring into the screen. In a moment, he was alone. He ripped open the door and stepped out into the cooler air of the open church.

He staggered toward the altar. He needed to pray, thirsted for the meditative calmness that came when he communed with God. As his eyes fell on the Virgin Mary, fury gave way to lucidity.

A craven, desolate cold wrenched the fire from his belly. His knees buckled. Father Brown crashed to the ground, his conscience in agony—not the one belonging to the Church and Seal of Sacrament, but the deeper one, the truer one, the human one.

I know that voice. God help me, I know that man.

6

Ted Allen laid corpse-still on the California king bed, his naked body encased in high-count silk sheets and surrounded by several oversized, hand-sewn satin pillows filled with goose feathers. An aroma, subtle and sweet, provided by an ionized filter attached to the home's HVAC unit, filled his lungs with every breath, leaving an equally sweet taste tickling his throat. It reminded him of honeysuckle.

Though the rest of him lay perfectly still, his penis, artificially imbued with vigor thanks to Viagra, bounced around, its vertical smile taunting him. Impotence would've been a relief.

Play your role, you traitorous bastard, play your role.

The click of his wife unhooking the first of an untold number of snaps on her bodice pulled his attention. Her shoulders reflected the light from the vanity mirror.

My God, the woman is already sweating.

The deed was almost at hand. She would soon begin the slow walk toward him, in what she thought to be a most appealing fashion. She would sit at the foot of the bed between his legs and caress her body from her breasts, overflowing now that they were freed from bondage, down to her ever-ready. Foreplay would go on forever. The actual engagement would take even longer.

Ted grimaced inwardly. He stared at her back, meeting her eyes in the mirror's reflection. She smiled seductively; he reciprocated. Ted put his hands behind his head and looked up at the rotating, multicolored blades of the ceiling fan, counting the revolutions of the blue one. He would keep his eyes riveted to the fan until he felt her hands on his calves. That was the signal.

Close your eyes, Ted. Moan in appropriate intervals. When she lies on top of you, rub her back, softly at first, then hard, with just the right amount clawing, and at the end, like you're a crazed, raving sexual lunatic. Moan more. Make sure you grab her tits. Good God, she loves those damn things. When she finally straddles you, your work is done. She'll decide when you're finished.

Ted had begun repeating his personal instructions when the phone rang.

Ignore it, Ted. Remember to moan.

The phone went to voicemail and immediately started ringing again. He let it go to voicemail a second time. He could hear her making final preparations. His eyes were about to close when the ring resumed.

Goddammit. "What?" he grabbed the phone and shouted.

"Sorry, did I wake you?"

"What do you want?" Ted growled.

As he listened to one of his contacts inside the police department prattle on about a murder case, he became aware that his wife was already on the bed. She was halfway up his thighs.

No. No. Wait. Not ready.

"You called my house at this hour to tell me about some mob hit? Are you out of your mind?"

Ted listened further to the caller's story; as it progressed, he became less annoyed and more and more interested.

"Really?" he asked. "That many?"

Ted's better half now had both her hands wrapped around Viagra's production, stroking hard and fast. Ted covered the phone and mouthed, "One more minute, can't you see I'm on the phone?"

She smiled at him, nodded, and laid her hands on his thighs.

"Thank you," he mouthed.

"You're welcome," she replied and proceeded to take the entire thing that would not die into her mouth.

Bitch.

He ignored her lascivious slurping and concentrated on the information. It was good. It was really good.

"Oh yes, I know someone. I'll get it done first thing

in the morning. You've done well. I won't forget this."

Ted hung up the phone and tossed it aside. He was giddy. He almost didn't mind his wife in that moment.

She said something about being sorry for being rude, but he didn't pay her any attention. His mind whirled with the information and the possibility it afforded him. Ted closed his eyes, not in escapism now but in ecstasy. When he opened them, his wife was above him. Uncharacteristically, he traced his fingers along the line of her firm, muscular shoulders. He nuzzled his face against her jaw line, slightly too rigid for her soft features.

"You know what?" he said, looking right into her eyes, "You're goddamn beautiful."

And as he turned the tables and positioned himself behind her, all the while keeping a tight grip on her shoulders, Ted didn't close his eyes one time.

7

The irregular rhythm of the shower was exasperating. One second a frigid dribble fell straight down, and the next, a powerful, scalding stream pelted against her—hard and hot enough to force her to step back.

Rosalind Williams turned the water off after a few minutes, escaping with just a slight burn on her upper back and emerging from the small restroom a short time later fully dressed.

Uncle Willie—who wasn't an uncle, or related at all for that matter—stood in the hall outside the door. The tattered robe he wore was agape, and he had his ever-present twenty-four ounce can of beer (today's selection Colt 45) in hand. A Kool cigarette, which managed to fling ash everywhere but on him, hung from his mouth.

"Rosie, how ya doin' dis mornin'? Gurl, I thought yo' ass was gon' be in der awl day."

"I'm fine, Willie. Excuse me."

Willie leaned against the wall and crisscrossed his feet one on the other, his hand resting on his Hanes, patting like he was trying to extinguish a fire.

"Gurl, I had heard ya yellin', thought ya mighta slipped and fell," he said.

"Nope, I'm fine. Excuse me."

Glassy eyes traveled the length of her body; acrid smoke surrounded her.

"Cuz if ya hada fell, that shit woulda hut."

Rosie clutched her clothes close to her chest and stepped over him, swiveling her hips as she tried to maneuver around Willie in the narrow hallway.

Willie had long arms.

Just as she cleared his outstretched legs, he grabbed a handful of her bottom. She kept walking, threw her clothes into her room, and hit the stairs in stride.

"Gurl, ya need ta quit playin' and gimme somma dat goodie," he yelled.

The sound of grease popping and the Delfonics on the radio welcomed her into the kitchen. Her mother, in the twin robe to Willie's—though not quite as tattered and cinched in the front—stood over the stove, flipping bacon and stirring a pot of grits.

Mama sang along loudly, tone deaf, but with veritable passion as she rocked to the beat.

"Morning, Mama."

Mama wasn't finished having her mind blown and found an even higher octave.

Rosie sat down at the table. She put her head in her hands and blew out a long, exaggerated sigh.

"Got sometin ta say?" Mama asked between belting

out lyrics.

"No, Mama."

"Uh-huh. You betta put dem eyes back in yo' head 'fo I do it fo' ya."

Rosie hadn't been rolling her eyes before, but she did now. She fingered her grandmother's charm bracelet and tried to remember better days. The image was foggy and distant, the soothing sound of her grandmother's voice overrun by the dull drumming of her present.

Mama put the plate in front of her. It hit with a thud.

"Hur."

The bacon was black and curled, crispy to the point of being brittle. A mountainous heaping of salt and pepper covered the grits. The eggs, cooked in *old* grease, were full of bits of bygone meals.

She stuffed a piece of burnt toast into her mouth.

Willie strolled into the kitchen. He crumpled the beer can and threw it in the trash. He sashayed behind Mama, grabbed her hips, and grinded against her.

"Ooooh," Mama said.

"Whatcha call me, baby?" he asked, nibbling on her ear.

"Sweet dick Willie," she replied.

"Ya damned righ'," Willie said, turning to wink at Rosie.

She lost what little appetite she had and spit the toast into a napkin.

"What's good, Unc? Hey, Mama." Rosie's younger brother, Marcus, came in, reeking of marijuana.

"Shid, lil nigga, ya know hah I do."

"Hey, baby, bre'fis be ready inna minute," Mama said.

Marcus took the seat next to Rosie. He mussed his hand through her dreadlocked hair.

"Damn, girl, when you gon' cut dat shit? Walkin' 'round lookin' like doo doo head uh some shit."

It wasn't funny or original, but Willie and Marcus laughed like it was the first time they'd heard it, not the hundredth.

"Lil girl," Mama said, turning to face her, "I done tole yo' ass ya need ta cut dat shit out cho head. Hah you think dem white folk look'a yo' ass, witcha lookin' all crazy by da head? Dats why yo' high siddity ass got fured in da firs' place."

Rosie didn't respond. She could've pointed out that, regardless of her hairstyle, she was the only person in the house with a job. Strangely, she wasn't, however, the only person with an income. Every month two disability payouts and a Social Security check for Willie's mother, who Rosie figured was dead or wished she was, found their way into the mailbox.

She checked the time and mentally counted the minutes until her cab arrived. That honk was the best part of her day.

The doorbell rang instead.

Willie and Marcus didn't move an inch. They continued their conversation like nothing had happened. Mama brought a platter of bacon and all the fixings to the table.

"I know you ain't deaf," she said to Rosie while chewing vigorously.

Rosie had reached her limit for family time this morning. Her eyes stung by the time she reached the front door. When she opened it, a gust of cold air and the sight on the porch dried any oncoming tears. On the stoop, the most pleasing thing she'd seen all morning met her bewildered look with a blinding smile. The man wore a simple black suit that looked painted on; it hugged in all the right places.

"Ms. Rosalind Williams?" he asked.

She blinked several times, trying to figure out the right answer. "Y-y-yes. I'm Rosalind."

The family had congregated behind her in the hallway.

"Who dat be?" Marcus shouted.

"Ms. Williams, my employer would like a word with you."

The man gestured behind him. Double parked in the street idled a car five hundred times too expensive for the neighborhood.

"Dayum, look at dat shit," Marcus said.

"He has a business proposition he believes will interest you."

Rosie had several questions to ask the attractive man; chiefly, who was this employer and what did he want with her?

Marcus spoke before she could. "Gah damn, dat

nigga got a May-back. Haaa, I tole ya'll she bin slangin' dat pussy on da low."

"Teasin' azz bitch," Willie added.

Rosie stepped out and closed the door behind her before she could hear Mama's disapproving agreement.

8

The man stared intently at the houses. He logged and categorized every detail in separate files inside his head. File #457 Whispering Hollow Court: one occupant, female, 40-50 years old. She drove a small, rear-wheel-drive car; the oil-smeared tire tracks in the driveway were close together. The burnout was darkest at the back of the reverse swerve into the street, and on and on. File #459 Whispering Hollow Court was equally full.

He didn't try to do it. His mind just worked in a certain way. In the same way Bob Dylan wrote songs or Van Gogh painted, this man noticed minutiae. Once a doctor had said he had an eidetic memory. The doctor was obviously wrong, because for the life of him, the man couldn't recall the doctor's name.

He shut his eyes and rubbed his forehead. He was reluctant to admit it, but he was disappointed. The dark circles under his eyes made that impossible to ignore. The conversation had not gone as planned. He hadn't really *expected* the priest to give his blessing, but Father Brown's condemnation was a shock.

Father, how can you be so obtuse?

A fitful night of soul searching had left the man tired and moody. No matter, Father Brown would realize the error of his judgment.

The light of truth shines brighter than the abyss of liars and fools.

He sighed and picked up his things. He walked up to the front door of the house just as it swung open. A fat, troll-like man stood before him.

"Good morning to you. I'm looking for a Mr. Hollis Anderson," he said, looking down at his clipboard.

"Yep, you got him," the troll answered. "And just so you know, whatever you're selling, I ain't buying."

"Don't be so hasty, Mr. Anderson. These here are hand-polished and decorated by a great group of children down at Liberty Mission for Battered Women. I'll give you one free of charge. If you'd like to donate, we take linens, nonperishables, and toiletries."

"Whoa, whoa. I guess you weren't listening. I ain't buying shit," Hollis responded.

The man held one of the crafts, a polished and painted stone about the size of a softball, aloft.

"That's cute," Hollis said derisively. "I could give a shit about the battered women of whatever or their stupid brats. Bitch shoulda kept her mouth shut."

Hollis sneered at the man on his porch. The man glanced around a few seconds. When he turned back to Hollis, he shot his hand forward so fast the sneer hadn't left Hollis's mouth when the stone smashed into it.

Hollis staggered back into his house. The man heaved the crate of crafts onto his hip and stepped inside. He kicked a few of Hollis's teeth back into the foyer and closed the door behind him.

"What the fuck?" Hollis screamed while trying to regain his footing.

Why do they always say that? the man wondered. *What do you mean what the fuck? I just knocked out half your teeth; that's the fuck.*

The man stood casually in the entryway and reached into the crate. Hollis was standing now. He took a step forward. In retrospect, he would think he should've taken that step the other way.

As it was, Hollis went at the intruder.

Because the bastard hit me in my damn mouth, in my damn house. He's a big boy, but I'm a bigger goddamn boy. And he's in my goddamn house!

When that first stone hit his hip and he felt bones break in a way he didn't think possible, accompanied by a pain that nearly made him pass out, he knew just how bad a call he had made. When stone number four felled him again, this time permanently, he just wished for a quick end. The barrage was unyielding. Hollis lost count after nine. No part of him was left untouched by the stoning, save his face.

"Do you remember their names?" the man asked as he stood over Hollis.

"Please, please don't do this. I don't know any names. What are you talking about? Please, oh

Jesus," he said, wheezing because his ribs were poking through his lungs by this point.

"Is that what they said?" the man asked.

He lifted another larger stone high above his head, casting a shadow over his face.

"'He shall surely be put to death; all the congregation shall certainly stone him'," the man said, his voice clear and calm.

In that instant, Hollis remembered who the man was and the names he wanted, an answer forever silenced by a giant, polished stone.

A short time later, the man sat in Hollis's garage inside Hollis's car, preparing to leave when he saw something amiss with File #457 Whispering Hollow Court. The shadows inside didn't belong. Shards of broken glass along the side of the house glimmered brightly in the morning sun, inviting him.

The man checked his watch and clipboard.

"I have time," he said with a genuine smile.

9

Rosie settled into the supple leather backseat, and her Adonis walked around to the driver's side. As the car pulled away, she sat quietly, as one who had been beckoned.

Her host was shielded behind a newspaper. He'd given no indication that he knew or cared that she was there. A few blocks later, he folded the newspaper into his lap and regarded her.

"You know, these things are mostly filled with drivel," he said.

Rosie's heart thumped in her ears. She tightened her jaw and clenched her fists so hard her fingernails dug into her palm.

"I mostly read it for entertainment, but every so often, a piece of real news makes it in there, and I learn something. You?"

Words flooded her brain, jostling to be the first uttered. "Ted Allen."

She shook her head, furious at everyone in the car, including herself.

"Ted Allen," she said again. "How dare you?"

"How dare I what?"

"Stop this car," she shouted, turning to Ted's driver.

"Keep going, Luis," Ted said.

The car moved steadily through traffic. Rosie spun back around to face Ted. He met her anger with a serenity that infuriated her even more.

"How dare you? You show up to my home? You bastard!" Rosie screamed, not in fear or anger, but in exasperation. It was all too much—Willie, Marcus, Mama, and *now* Ted Allen. She couldn't take it. Tears flowed down her cheeks.

"You finished?" he asked.

She glared at him silently.

"Good," he said, taking this as an affirmation. "You need to calm down. Only one of us in this car had to spend millions defending accusations against their businesses and their person. Only one of us had to deal with city officials, state, and then federal prosecutors all trying to make a name taking down Ted Allen. Only one of us should be angry, and I've gotten over it."

Rosie suddenly felt like she was falling. She grabbed the seat and took several deep breaths. Steadied, she looked into Ted's face. *I can't believe it. That son of a bitch actually looks pained. Is this real? What the hell is happening?*

"Why am I so angry?" she asked. "You, you destroyed my life. I live with my *mother*!"

Ted couldn't help but smile at her disdain. "You did

this to yourself. Groundless accusations of bribery, embezzlement, political corruption. Come now, take responsibility for your actions. If you'd bothered to get my side of the story, I would've shown you how wrong you were."

"I wasn't wrong. What I wrote was the truth," she shouted.

He shrugged his shoulders. "Be that as it may, you *did* write it. Didn't anyone ever tell you, 'Threaten down, never up'? 'Cause when you do, all the shit lands right on your head."

The look of pity in his eyes was coupled with a sincere smile. Rosie was undone. She'd cried, she'd screamed, she'd accused. The only thing left was to stare dumbfounded at this man who, with a few phone calls to his buddies, had effectively submarined her career.

"What do you want?" she asked.

"Exactly. No use looking backward," he said, patting her leg.

Rosie wanted to cringe, but she was just too damned tired. Ted reached down and produced a leather briefcase. He handed it to her.

"Open it."

She looked at the pages and photos inside. Every one caused her eyes to widen a little more, another layer of anger replaced by curiosity.

"I presume you've heard about these?" he asked.

Enthralled, Rosie nodded, her attention fully on the pages in the briefcase. Ted reached across and closed the lid. Hard.

She jumped back, a little afraid. He glared at her until she eased back into her seat.

"Very well then, as you undoubtedly already know, ten people were killed yesterday. Now for what you don't: Actually, there were fifteen. The police framed the last one as a tragic accident. A collapsed house made the story credible, and the news ran with it. What the police didn't say was that three of the people were shot, and the last two were buried alive in the rubble. Tied down and buried alive."

Rosie didn't have to feign interest. She was completely absorbed. She knew something good was coming.

"They were all killed by the same man."

Ted let that last sentence hang in the air as he watched her. He could see the wheels turning, could feel the shift in atmosphere.

"How do you know that?"

"I know because I do," he said, as if that answer were sufficient.

"A serial killer," she said, a thought she hadn't meant to utter.

Ted gave her a look that suggested she'd said something cute, but not quite smart.

"Serial killer? No, no. Dahmer was a serial killer. Berkowitz, Bundy, those were serial killers. What we have here is something else. We have a messenger."

Rosie wanted to understand. She hated to look incapable in front of anyone, especially *him*, but she didn't have it all. And he knew it.

Smug son of a bitch.

"Okay, I'll bite," she said. "What's the message?"

Rosie became aware that the car had stopped. She looked around, trying to get her bearings; the area seemed vaguely familiar. Then, looking outside the parking garage, she saw the sign: *St. Lo..s Da..y Gaze..e.*

"That is for you to ascertain. I trust a mind as sharp as yours will have no trouble figuring out what to write."

She looked down at the briefcase in her lap. There it was: her marching orders.

Can I? Should I?

"Why me? I'm sure there are people, better credentialed people who could do it."

"You should give yourself more credit."

Her response, a dubious stare, did nothing to sway Ted's confidence.

"Take, for example, that eviscerating exposé on yours truly—what was it called? 'Ted Allen: Robber Baron for A New Century'? Although it was your work, and thusly your fault, maybe my legal team went a little overboard on you."

He paused. Then he reached into a cooler and produced two flutes—one with champagne, the other with orange juice. As he combined them he glanced at her, almost begging her to fill the silence. She knew it was a calculated respite. She wouldn't take the bait.

"So I feel partly responsible for the predicament

you find yourself in, living with your mother and struggling to eke out an existence at the puff piece you presently call a job."

"Why me?" she asked again.

Ted was incredulous. Rosie was unmoved by his heartfelt mea culpa. Magnanimity, apparently, would not rule the day.

"Fine. We both know you're very good, *and* we both know you couldn't be farther from my first choice. However, the Daily Gazette does have a certain...shall we say, editorial leniency that suits me."

"And I give you a certain level of plausible deniability if this blows up in my face," she added.

Ted smiled. He might actually like her one day.

The scent of marijuana from Rosie's shirt wafted into her nose. The thought of Willie's lecherous yearnings and the barely concealed hatred Mama felt for her first born prickled her skin in goosebumps. The sound of her grandmother's voice, *Baby, sometimes you gotta pay yo' dues,* came through loud and clear.

Rosie mumbled something to herself.

"Excuse me?"

"Mr. Allen, if I were to do this, I would want—"

Ted held his hand up. He patted hers atop the briefcase.

"I don't give a shit what you want. This is the deal. You cost me millions. Despite that, I'm handing you the keys to the story of a lifetime. Hell, I'm your fairy godmother. You take it, you do what I say when I say. You don't, you don't. There's no middle ground called *what Rosie wants.*"

Rosie thought for just a second. She thanked Luis for the ride and got out. She walked over to the elevator and waited for it to arrive as the car passed behind her. She didn't look back; it didn't slow.

Only once she was in the privacy of the elevator did Rosie manage to breathe again. She tore open the envelope Ted had put on her hand when he patted it.

The cashier's check was for twenty-thousand dollars. The sticky note attached to the front said: DO NOT SCREW THIS UP.

Four years ago when Ted had wrecked her life, she'd been making little more than that. Rosie leaned back against the wall and exhaled.

Baby, ain't nothing in this world free. Be sho you can pay the man when the bill come due.

"I already paid, Grandmama. I already paid."

[END OF PART I]

PART II:
10

Detective Pat McConnell stood outside Conference Room B feeling like he'd been hit by a truck. Two hours of sleep, three crime scenes full of evidence that pointed everywhere and nowhere, and an unreasonable amount of Jägermeister had left him surlier than usual. Lou's interminable great morning disposition didn't make it any better.

"Room B. This can't be good," Lou said.

Pat agreed. The motto of Conference Room B, nicknamed Alien, was "Go ahead and scream—no one can hear you." It was tucked in a lower-level, rarely traveled part of police headquarters where, in the old days, the aggressive interrogations had taken place. Nowadays, it was the officers themselves who feared Room B. A lot of careers went there to die.

When the door opened, several uniformed officers walked out. Each one looked like he'd just been told he had inoperable cancer.

"Well, this ain't good," Lou said.

"You notice that?" Pat asked.

"Yep, all the guys from yesterday."

"Detectives, come in. Shut it behind you," a voice called from inside.

Lou and Pat walked into the conference room to find Chief of Police Brian James and Deputy Mayor Chris Watson seated at the end of a long table. Around it were Pat and Lou's direct superior, Detective Sergeant Nathan Davis, and a smattering of white shirts, captains, and lieutenants. Off to the side stood a man Pat didn't know, though he knew *what* he was. Brooks Brothers suit, hair cut high and tight, an air of authority: Fed.

Circlin' the wagons, eh, fellas? Pat thought.

"Detectives Pat McConnell and Lou Maguire," Chief James introduced. "This is Special Agent Jason Manin. You know everyone else."

They sat. A glare and clenched jaw conveyed every ounce of distaste Pat had for the marriage of police and politics.

"Now, gentlemen, we expressed our wishes that this matter stay out of the media to the others. I hope you two don't require that particular speech."

"Chief, we know the score," Pat said. "With all due respect, sir, let's not dick around. How 'bout we get the cards on the table."

Only Chief James and Lou, both well-versed in Pat-speak, were unmoved by his outburst.

"Go ahead. Deal 'em, McConnell," Chief James said.

"All the vics were done by the same guy," Pat

began. "Eight were ventilated by an identical high-powered rifle, three took .44 shells to the face, and four got a special send-off. Now, tell us something we don't know."

Chief James gestured to Agent Manin. "You heard the man; what don't we know?"

"First of all," Agent Manin said, "I'm here only in an advisory capacity. The FBI only wants to assist you in apprehending the UNSUB."

"Meaning it's too messy right now, so let the PD take the heat, and you guys can swoop in later, looking like white knights. Yeah, we got it," Pat said.

"Yep. Got that right," Lou added.

"Gentleman," Chief James said. "Be quiet."

Agent Manin thanked the chief, who met him with a dismissive wave.

"Yes, Detective McConnell, all the victims were killed by the same UNSUB. What you don't know is what connects them. Obviously we have a serial, and they all like a particular type. And in this, gentlemen, you share a commonality with him. Every single victim has spent an appreciable amount of time involved with the justice system."

Pat and Lou exchanged knowing and bored glances.

No shit, Sherlock, Pat thought. "So, not choirboys. You gonna tell us something useful or can we get back on the street?"

"So you're saying it's a cop," Davis said. "Maybe one of the guys we talked to before. I knew we should've grilled 'em harder."

"It's not a cop," Pat said.

"Really? Sounds like a cop to me. Chief, we gotta real problem on our hands," Davis countered.

"Jumped on that kinda quick didn't ya, Sarge?"

"You got something you wanna say, McConnell?" Davis asked.

"Gentleman, please," the chief boomed. "Agent Manin, will you get on with it!"

"Of course, Chief. No, Sergeant, the detective is most likely correct. Our profile suggests the UNSUB is a white male between the ages of thirty and forty-five, well educated—probably extremely so, a military background, lives alone, most likely never married, and now works, or did at some point recently, in *some* area of law enforcement."

"That's not much," Lou offered. "You're talking about a couple thousand people."

"I know, Detective. I've only had this for a few hours. I'll be able to offer more—"

"When more stiffs start rolling in," Pat finished.

Agent Manin simply shrugged.

"What about the special send-offs a few of 'em got?" Lou asked.

"Clearly some type of message. I don't know the whys, but educated guess right now...they were more personal to him."

The room was quiet, each man consumed by his own thoughts. One was clear headed.

"Is that the best you've got? Wait for more bodies

to show up? I have to say I'm underwhelmed," Deputy Mayor Watson said.

The chief's raised hand muted the response he knew was coming from Pat. The exchange didn't go unnoticed.

"Just so we're clear, people," Watson said, his words directed at Pat, "if we find out any of you talked to anyone outside this room, you will feel the full weight of City Hall crashing down on you. I give you my word; I will end you."

He held Pat's gaze a moment longer before directing his comments to the others.

"That is not an idle threat. The mayor's office cannot, I repeat, *cannot* have the people of this city worried that a serial killer is on the loose."

"Election years are a bitch," Pat said.

Watson ignored him. He turned to Chief James.

"Brian, you've done good work. We've been very appreciative. Crime is down across the board, but this sort of thing, if it were to get out... Well, just clean it up quickly and quietly. Remember, no one is irreplaceable."

He gazed around the room, meeting every man's eyes, in a few cases finding them downcast. He gave Chief James a curt nod and stood to leave.

"True words, *no one* is irreplaceable," Pat added.

Deputy Mayor Watson froze in the doorway. Without turning, he said, "Brian, get your dog on a leash or put him down."

He slammed the door, causing it to spring back

open.

"Close the damn door," Chief James said. "McConnell, your fight is with the asshole chopping up people in my city. If you can't get a handle on that, I will remedy your situation this very instant."

Pat's response was interrupted by a petrified young officer, who barged in cradling a laptop like it was radioactive.

"Son, what part of private is confusing to you? *Get* or *the fuck out?*"

"I'm sorry, Chief, but you gotta see this," the officer said.

The man put the laptop on the table and backed out as fast as he'd come in.

The men huddled around the screen.

"Sweet Jesus, Mary, and Joseph," Lou said.

"FUBAR," Pat said.

The white shirts shot wondering glances at each other and accusing glares at the two detectives. Chief James put his head in his hands. He knew his vacant office was alive with a belligerent phone's ringing.

A loud screech pulled their attention to the doorway. Deputy Mayor Watson stood just inside the room, looking unhinged.

"Which one of you mealy-mouthed sons of bitches did this?" he shouted.

11

"St. Louis Arch Angel," Ted said. "A little on the nose, I think."

"You gave me a lot to digest this morning. I thought it was pretty good on short notice," Rosie responded.

Ted said nothing. He let the silence hang in the air and buzz through the phone line. The sound was deafening, a chisel and hammer chipping away at her false veneer.

"Mr. Allen, I can change it before the article goes to print," she offered meekly.

"That may be for the best. I'll give it some thought."

Her stuttering questions were ended by the click of the receiver. Ted interlocked his fingers and placed his hands against his chin, regarded by Luis.

"Sir, you seemed to like it, or did I misread you?" Luis asked.

Ted rotated his chair toward the fireplace, which cast his face in an orange hue. The flames, reflected in the bottoms of his glasses, leaped toward his eyes in perpetual eagerness to devour him.

"I do."

Luis asked no more, as years ago, he too had been given a version of the "no middle ground called *what you want*" speech. Therefore, he was concerned with Rosalind Williams, and his own curiosity, to exactly the extent Ted required.

When the phone rang, he looked at his boss. A wave of Ted's hand answered his question. He picked up the phone and listened.

"Front desk. He's downstairs," Luis said after he hung up.

"Good. Show him in."

"Yes, sir."

He left Ted alone with his thoughts, and what glorious thoughts they were. The game was afoot, and in the game, Ted was without peer. He had made his first several million at twenty-two. It hadn't been quite legal or ethical, but then money wasn't stamped with the words *earned through hard, law-abiding, ethical means.*

He'd learned a couple valuable lessons the day he convinced his much older, supposedly more seasoned partners that the sale of their early-iteration instant messaging software for seventy-five thousand was the best they could get. One, making money was exhilarating, but it paled in comparison to the game. Two, most men are concerned with either self-preservation or self-respect, and both can be exploited. Ted was saddled with neither compunction. He was concerned with winning.

I'd kick Bobby Fisher's ass.

Ted was a fair chess player. He had the mind to be a wonderful player, but there was just something innately boring about a game of marble horses and castles; there was no *real* incentive to win. No actual gains or losses, life or death.

Death the zenith, birth the opportunity. The rest was a labyrinth of dead-ends, a bloodthirsty Minotaur, cowards and fools, the weak and the strong. *Life* was the only game that mattered.

In the hours since he'd recruited Rosie, Ted hadn't had a sip of alcohol. And yet he was nearing intoxication—sweaty upper lip, clammy palms, hazy vision. He was drunk on the insatiable lust of self-appointed great men: power. His solitary bender of personal aggrandizement was interrupted when the phone rang.

"John, how are you?" he answered.

"Thirty percent stake at *that* price? Who the hell do you think you are?"

"John, listen—"

"No, Ted, you listen. You think you can strong arm me? You think you're the only one who knows people? How about I tell you to take your *offer* and shove it up your ass? While I'm at it, I'll give Commissioner Gregg a call. The ethics committee would love another go at you."

"John, save that fire for the next board meeting. You're going to need it to convince them."

"Did you hear a word I said? Never going to

65

happen. Never."

"A black and red book embossed with a gold jasmine flower," Ted said slowly, letting each word hang.

He could hear John Keane, CFO of Heritage Insurance, frantically opening and closing desk drawers. It sounded like a whack-a-mole game. Ted rolled his eyes.

Idiot.

"Relax. When you deliver the board, you'll have a present waiting for you. You're not the only chef in town. Cooked books are aplenty. There's a certain investment company that I bet will be just falling all over themselves to give you the IPO price. Or, perhaps, you fancy dog food?"

"You're shitting me."

Ted didn't utter a sound. *Couple things, John, don't ever ask or answer a stupid question.*

"I'll be damned," John concluded after a moment. "You're serious."

"You feeling better now?"

"I could be worse."

"Saves me the trouble of pointing that out," Ted replied.

He hung up as Luis returned, trailed by another man.

"Widow Drake," Luis announced.

Luis didn't wait to be dismissed. He bowed low and scooted backward from the room. He was much larger than the man he'd escorted in. He was also trained well in various forms of self-defense and was an expert shot, yet he still couldn't wait to be out of Widow's presence.

Ted allowed himself a barely perceptible smirk and thought, *I don't blame you one bit.*

"Mr. Drake, have a seat."

The plainly dressed man walked to the chair. His steps were ghostlike, his movements reminiscent of a jungle cat. He sat down, crossed his legs, and leaned on one of the armrests, all without making a sound. Ted was sure if he closed his eyes, he'd have no reason to think he wasn't the only person in the room.

"Mr. Drake, there are things I need you to sort out. I'm sure you're unaware, but the city has had a sudden rash of—"

"I'm aware of the situation," he replied.

Ted's jaw clenched, his brow furrowed. For a fleeting moment, he was on the verge of chastising Widow. In the next, he recalled his sense and thought better of it.

"Very well, I need you to find out who's doing it."

A toothy beam lit up Widow's face. The cat was baring his teeth.

"Your concern is touching."

"Yes, it is."

"And when I find him?" he asked.

When not if. "Do nothing. Your job is to observe and report back," Ted said. He tossed a flash drive to Widow. "Everything you need to get started."

"And if nothing isn't possible?"

I do so love a maniac.

Ted reached into a drawer, producing a pistol.

"Use this."

Widow pocketed the drive and gun, turning to leave.

"Mr. Drake..." Ted said.

"Don't bother. I won't."

Ted ground his teeth and crumpled papers on his desk. He shouted for Luis, louder and more aggressively than he had to. His assistant threw open the door and rushed inside, hand poised over his hip. Before Luis realized there was no emergency, Widow had whirled to face him, crouched in a shooter's stance.

"Your ass better have an itch you're just *dying* to scratch," Widow said.

Luis froze, save his knees, which shook hard enough that Ted could hear keys jingling in his pocket. Entranced by the big Luger pointed at his face, Luis's hand still lingered over his hip.

Ted saved his life.

"Luis, see our guest to the elevator."

Luis didn't so much straighten as he slumped, relief emanating off him in waves. Only when he relaxed did Widow react in kind and holster his gun. He walked over to Luis, very much at ease. Luis gave the smaller man a wide berth and fell in several steps behind.

He returned shortly, looking sallow.

"Is there something wrong, Luis?"

Luis glanced over his shoulder and whispered, "Drake."

Ted bit back a chuckle. Luis crossed himself.

"Luis, I must say I'm pleased. Such loyalty is a rare commodity today."

"Mr. Allen, sir, thank you, sir."

"Tell you what, it's been too long since your wife and children have seen you at the dinner table. Luis, take the rest of the day off."

At that, Luis regained much of his composure. He thanked Ted profusely, and his knees slowed their constant quake to a slight quiver.

"Think nothing of it, Luis. You've earned it."

He grabbed his things and headed for the door, thoughts of his kids' jubilant shouts hastening his steps.

"There's just one more thing I need before you go," Ted said.

Luis's body slammed into an invisible barrier, robbing him of motion, muting the joyful sounds of his children. But he swallowed his scowl and smiled; Ted Allen could hear your smile.

"Of course, sir," he said, dropping his bag at the entryway.

12

Alex Thomas woke with a start. He lay on his stomach, his hands and feet interlocked and tied ankle to wrist. His body felt run over—tractor trailer run over. His head throbbed, and with his one remaining good eye, he was seeing double. His breath snaked in a thin line through whatever part of his nose wasn't swollen or filled with clotted blood. The wet rag stuffed in his mouth made the chore infinitely more difficult.

A gash on his forehead, which he remembered was from the kitchen counter, oozed a perpetual stream of blood onto his face. In an ill-fated attempt to clear his vision, Alex shook his head. He was rewarded with a mind-numbing stab of pain and almost passed out.

He held on, barely. Eschewing any thoughts of visual clarity, he laid his head back on the floor. He rubbed globs of the blinding blood off on the soaked carpet and tried to focus.

He could see a pair of black shoes in the kitchen. A man walked backward, swiping Alex's mop across the tile. He hummed a tune while he worked. Alex knew the song; it was one his mother used to sing when *she* mopped the same floor.

Oh happy day, Oh happy day, Oh happy, happy day! Oh happy day when Jesus washed.

He yelled through the rag and strained against his bonds. The effort caused him exquisite pain and somehow tightened the knots, leaving him in more discomfort.

The man in the kitchen paused long enough to turn and look at Alex on the floor. Even above the constant chainsaw buzzing in his head, Alex heard the man chuckle at him.

In a furious state he was sure would somehow grant him the strength to bust out of the bindings and kick the mother's-song-stealing cocksucker in the ass, he struggled harder and screamed louder, rocking his body to and fro. Pain soon stole his vigor and consciousness.

When he woke again, the man had finished the kitchen and most of the family room. It seemed every inch of his apartment would be disinfected. The man was now pouring bleach on blood splatters on the carpet. Alex's pain had settled into a manageable dullness.

"Pain is just weakness leaving the body," he'd often informed groups of wide-eyed preteens at his wrestling camp. They'd hung on his every word. "Once you get past the shock, it's just like a two-day-old bruise."

That may have been a bit of an overstatement, but

thinking it, he felt better nonetheless. The rag in his mouth had almost dried and now allowed for more air to get in *and* out.

"Argh. You stupid cocksucker. You little bitch. Take off these ties or I will kick your ass," he shouted.

The man ignored him initially, apparently intent on bleaching the entire carpet. Only when he was finished did he kneel next to Alex and pat him on the head.

"Ugh," Alex groaned.

"You certainly put up quite the fight. I admit, I almost wasn't ready for it," the man said.

Alex craned his neck and levied all his anger at the man, though muffled profanities and attempted headbutts were his only weapons.

The man straddled him. Alex cursed and struggled against him, clenching his butt cheeks together.

"You faggot, get off me."

The man said something, but Alex didn't hear because as the man grabbed his right hand, a commercial for *CSI* came on the television, and for some reason, he paid attention.

When the man pried open his hand, holding his pinky finger erect, a disturbing thought occurred to Alex: his earlier futile attempt to fight back and the four red lines across the man's neck it had left behind.

The truth of the mopping, the bleach, and the grip that presently held one of his fingers upright drained him of bluster and rage. Only the hollow comprehension of his reality—beaten and hogtied at the mercy of a man who meant to do him considerable harm before killing him—remained.

Tears fell from his good eye. A whimper very like those that had given him so much satisfaction after he'd lied to those boys, said it wouldn't hurt and it did, said if they told anyone he'd kill their mommies and daddies, fell pitifully from his lips—until his sure-handed captor worked the blade with the precision of a surgeon and his pinky was no more, then he screamed.

The man lined up all five of Alex's fingers right in front of his face, like a hand coming up from a grave, before depositing them into a plastic baggy. Then he leaned forward and whispered into Alex's ear. When he stood, Alex saw him take something from his jacket—two sticks connected by a length of razor wire: a garrote.

He was grateful. He was ready.

After a few seconds, when the man hadn't moved, Alex yelled at him. He waited, wanted for several seconds, but still nothing.

Alex laughed and mumbled, his mind cracking into a million pieces. The man ignored his babbling and walked over to the television, turning it up.

"We have Michelle Bard at police headquarters with some information on a story first reported by News7," the anchor announced. *"Michelle?"*

"Yes, Bob," the reporter responded. *"Just a short while ago I had a chance to speak with Police Chief Brian James."*

The broadcast cut to tape of the interview.

"Chief James, what can you tell us about the so-called Arch Angel?"

"No comment."

"Chief, are you saying there is no Arch Angel?"

"No comment."

"Sources inside City Hall have alleged that the case is being mishandled and the leaks are coming from your department," the reporter continued. *"Any comment?"*

"The investigation is ongoing."

"Chief James, reports indicate that all fifteen murders were committed by the same person. Any truth to that?"

"To my knowledge," the chief replied, *"at this time, there is no confirmation of fifteen murders yesterday. The investigation is ongoing."*

The interview continued, but the man had evidently heard enough. He turned the volume down and paced the apartment in a slow circle, muttering to himself, while Alex, seemingly forgotten, watched in agony.

After a long time, the man stopped and knelt, facing Alex.

"Arch Angel it is," he said, and finally gave Alex relief.

13

Pat leaned against the car, standing in half-a-pack worth of discarded cigarette butts with a fresh one burning in his hand. Lou sat inside the car, stuffing leftovers from last night's dinner into his mouth.

The detectives were silent, each looking in a different direction, eyes glued to security-coded doors. Lou's opened first.

"There she is, chief."

Pat glanced over and spied the woman walking toward them. His stomach flipped. He clenched. It flipped more.

Her picture did not look like that.

"Man, she looks like a young Maureen," Lou said.

He regretted it the moment the words left his mouth, more so when Pat glared down into the car. Lou was sure a litany of Pat-isms was forthcoming, but the woman reached them first.

"Rosalind Williams, we need a word with you," Pat said, flipping out his badge.

Rosie backed against the wall, her expression worried.

"Am I under arrest?"

"No, Ms. Williams, but you need to come with us."

The surprise of ambush began to wane. The information from the files flooded her head.

Pat McConnell. And that makes you Lou Maguire, she thought.

Rosie was fully aware of what they wanted to talk about, and equally aware they couldn't compel her to say anything.

"I don't think so, Detective."

Pat glanced back at Lou and mouthed "Told ya." Lou shrugged.

"Ms. Williams," Pat said, producing an envelope, "we just want to talk to you. If you can't see it in your heart to have a conversation, my partner and I will leave you be."

He paused long enough to take an extended drag from the cigarette. Rosie thought it reminiscent of that morning's mimosa episode with Ted.

"And later tonight, when you're at home, my partner and I will execute this warrant. Marcus Williams and Eugene William Hanks, two felons, live on those premises, and though I'm sure they've cleaned up their acts, we will search every inch of that apartment. If we find anything, all of you are going to jail. Your choice."

Rosie did a poor job of masking her rage. She strode to the cruiser and snatched the door open. The door ground against the sidewalk, scraping deep gouges in the metal. She shot a satisfied look at Pat

REVELATION AND RETRIBUTION

and slammed it shut.

Eerily reminiscent indeed. Go to Hell, Pat McConnell.

Pat sat in the passenger seat, stuffed his gas bill back into his pocket, and turned to face her.

"Interesting article you wrote today."

"Thanks, I thought so."

"You wanna tell us how you came by your information?"

"I got it from the First Amendment."

Rosie allowed herself a big grin. She was proud of that quip.

"Hah, amendment my ass. See, me and my partner have a few theories. You wanna hear them?"

Pat lit another cigarette, waiting for her reply. She sat stone-faced. He inhaled deeply and blew the smoke into the backseat.

Oh, that's cold, Lou thought.

"One, somehow you got your pretty little hands on some stuff you weren't supposed to. Fine, whatever. But then you write your little piece and post it online, so now you're interfering with an ongoing investigation, a murder investigation. Sounds like obstruction to me. You, Lou?"

"Sounds about right there, chief."

Rosie almost laughed aloud. She was young, not stupid.

On second thought, you, sir, are no Ted Allen.

"Not sure the Supreme Court would agree," she countered. "Look, Detective, I'm just doing my job.

There were fifteen people killed yesterday by the same person. The public has a right to know."

"Yeah, thought you might say that. 'Member, we had two theories, and trust me, you're gonna wanna hear this one."

Rosie suddenly couldn't get comfortable. She shifted in the seat to no avail. The detective seemed too relaxed. When she'd worked for the *real* newspaper, The Post-Dispatch, the police had tried that obstruction line on several of her colleagues. It never worked, and nothing ever came of it, but it was always their go-to line. The fact that he so casually glossed over it worried her.

"See, you wrote about things only a few people outside this car know. And I checked—our files are intact; nothing's missing. Imagine my surprise when I saw that. Now don't get me wrong, leaks happen, but lady, the next day? Not likely."

"What's your point, Detective?" she asked.

"You're a writer, right? I mean, basically like a novelist or something. You know, you make shit up."

Rosie let the insult pass. He was messing with her, and they both knew it.

Just get to the damn point, she thought.

"Hey, Lou, what's that magic genie thing writers talk about? You know, the thing that tells them the story?"

"It's called a muse," Rosie said before she could stop herself.

Pat snapped his fingers, clapped Lou on the

shoulder, and gave Rosie a thumbs-up.

"Yep, that's right, the muse. So, we're figuring after we can't find any files missing, that you found out some other way. Like from a *muse*."

"What are you suggesting?"

The playfulness left Pat's demeanor. His face went rigid, his eyes hard and accusing.

"You know damn well. I think you talked to the man himself. You know details only the killer and we know. Since we haven't said squat to you, that leaves door number one. And you know what's behind door number one? Accessory after the fact, and you *can* take that to the Supreme Court."

Rosie regarded the detective through a relentless stream of secondhand smoke. He was angry. Even when he was playing the good cop, she could see it in his face. He was angry at her. She was happy to reciprocate.

"Detective, my sources are confidential, and I don't have to tell you a damn thing. But I will. I haven't met the man, but if I had, I'd shake his hand and say thank you."

"Fond of serial killers, are you?"

Rosie did laugh this time, loud and obnoxious. Lou whipped around and shushed her, pointing to his Bluetooth earpiece. Rosie's face softened, and she gestured to him. She *was* sorry.

"Hollow Court. Got it," he said in a Lou Maguire whisper, meaning you could hear him in the car next to them.

When she turned back to face Pat, she saw a mirrored scowl.

"Fifteen people were killed yesterday, who among them had been arrested eighty-seven times," she said. "*Eighty-seven.* Murder, manslaughter, rape, drug dealing, breaking and entering, assault, extortion, et cetera, et cetera. Serial killer? I'd call that civic duty, and I think your law-abiding citizens are sleeping a little more soundly tonight, don't you?"

"I think you could give a damn about the public. I think you got your ass spanked a few years ago, and you see this as your way back in."

Rosie was silent. Pat was content to fill the void.

"Oh yeah, we know all about you. You're a piss-ant reporter writing for a piss-ant paper, and you got ahold of something too big for your britches. And whoever got you into this, whether it's the man himself or God knows who else, is gonna hang you out to dry. And when they do, I'm gonna come see you again, 'cept I won't be so nice then. So, you stop what you're doing right now and tell me how you came by classified information or...I'll see you soon."

Lou looked at both of them, overcome by a feeling of déjà vu.

"Nine-five-four," Rosie began. She smirked condescendingly at Pat and then rattled off four more numbers.

The recitation took both detectives by surprise, though Pat was too angry to be speechless.

"What the hell is that?"

"My phone number. Whenever you get the urge to threaten me again, use it. I'll carve out an hour for you."

"Stop the car," Pat said.

Rosie waited patiently for Pat to let her out. She thanked Lou for the ride, which he reciprocated, and smiled sweetly at Pat as he held the door. She stood face to face with him for an instant before brushing past him, unfazed by his glower. Her smirk had yet to falter when their cruiser sped up the street.

You, sir, are no Ted Allen.

14

"If you happen to be unsure of your test, you've yet to face it. When that day arrives—and it will, dear friends—I pray your house is built not on the steel foundations of man but upon the rock of our Lord," Father Brown said in summation at evening mass.

He exited the pulpit and met his parishioners. He shook hands with each man and embraced every woman in a warm, platonic hug. He tousled the boys' hair and flipped the bills of their ever-present Cardinals baseball caps. He knelt eye to eye with all the pig-tailed, pea-coated girls and told every one of them she was the prettiest.

Then he met with Sister Mary Agnes, head of the convent, to discuss the upcoming charity drive. She had a plethora of wild ideas, each in more need of God's divine help than the last. The priest listened, laughing when appropriate, pondering and saddened when necessary, guiding her the entire time.

Father Brown left Sister Mary Agnes with a much more manageable game plan, which he was only too happy to let her take credit for, and retired to his tiny office.

When he stepped over the threshold, he hung up the charade of Father Brown, a pious and sure man of God, and sat down at the desk as Walter Brown, the haggard and fearful man grasping a bottle of merlot reserved for tortured souls.

He filled the glass and dialed the number. He was already in the motion of hanging up when the voicemail clicked on, again. Father Brown was on autopilot, numb before the first taste of red wine splashed down his throat.

Somewhere in his mind, a voice insisted that his private horror was just a nightmare, a fallacy concocted by demon spawn brought about to test his faith in the Almighty. Part of him ached to believe that.

In his heart, however, he knew. He'd known when he rose from bed, *rose* because there was no sleep for the priest; he could still hear the sure voice of the killer who'd visited the confessional. He'd understood after his morning coffee tasted like mud and his breakfast turned to ash in his mouth. When he'd opened the newspaper and his eyes floated over the blasphemous headline—*DOES ST. LOUIS HAVE AN ARCH ANGEL?*—his sobs and the unfathomable pain in his soul had removed all doubt. The test in faith was about *him.*

"Lord, why me?"

Every time he saw the headline, his eyes burned in anger, only to be quelled by tears of misery.

Invariably, he reached again for the bottle of merlot.

Arch Angel.

What was wrong with his people? The man who did these things was worthy of condemnation, not commendation. He'd said as much to his superior, Monsignor Horatio, when he'd gone to visit him earlier this afternoon. The Angel's voice had stolen even the peace of prayer from the priest, and solitude had become torturous.

"We don't condemn the man; we condemn the act," Monsignor Horatio replied.

"Monsignor, I've counseled scores of men and women over the years. I've heard every depraved desire, every despicable act. Do you know what real evil is? It isn't the bad man doing bad things; it's the man who does deplorable things because he's sure, intractably so, of the innate righteousness of his actions. This man...this man is evil. I know it in my heart."

Monsignor Horatio had started to respond—his mouth was literally open, ready for the words of rebuttal to spill forth—when the subtle admission in Father Brown's words reached his consciousness.

"The crisis of faith, it seems, *Father* Brown, lies not with the people of St. Louis, but with you," he said in measured tones.

"My faith in God is ever intact," Father Brown replied, defensively, reflexively.

"And your vows. We don't cast them aside when they become uncomfortable," Monsignor Horatio stated.

How? How has this turned? Father Brown lamented silently.

The conversation continued along the same lines for the remainder of their visit. The solace Father Brown sought would not be found here. However, thinly veiled threats were abundant. The monsignor didn't exactly say *excommunication*, but he needn't bother. Father Brown wanted very much to be angry with Monsignor Horatio for being simple-minded, but he knew full well that just a few days ago, had he been in Monsignor Horatio's place, he too would've draped himself in the impenetrable Seal of the Confessional. He, too, would have threatened his friend of thirty years because no force on Earth could compel a pious man to break God's law. And if that man is obliged to do so, he is no longer pious and must be discarded.

Until him.

Until now, even after five decades in the clergy, he'd never been *blessed* to be in the presence of true evil. Over the years, he'd ceased to be surprised at man's depravity, but ninety-nine percent of the horrible things he'd heard in the confessional would fall under the umbrella of the Cardinal Sins, and their perpetrators had come to repent. Now, with the sun down, he sat in his office, the hellish events of the last twenty-four hours replaying relentlessly, secure in the unholy knowledge that he'd met the one percent; and he had no idea what to do with it.

His face turned skyward. And there he stayed, the

wholeness of his mind, heart, and soul begging heaven for strength, for clarity, for answers.

An answer came in the form of the antique cuckoo clock hanging above his head. Father Brown steeled himself. He grabbed the old, worn Bible and the candlestick. He forced his feet to move, step by step, back into the darkened church, past the empty pews and under the tranquil gaze of the Son, to the confessional.

He stepped inside and turned on the green light outside, indicating a priest was present. As he sat, lit the candle, and flipped open the Bible, he was sure of two things.

First, he would start his night inside the confessional with Psalms 42:9-10: I will say to God my Rock, "Why hast thou forgotten me? Why go I mourning because of the oppression of the enemy? As with a sword in my bones, mine enemies reproach me; while they say daily unto me, Where is thy God?"

The second was confirmed when the voice, familiar *and* alien, spoke from beyond the barrier.

"Good evening, Father."

This night would be worse than the last.

15

Widow Drake drove his SUV down the alley across the street from the apartment building where Alex Thomas had been executed. He mounted a laser-scope microphone outside the passenger window and adjusted the direction. He plugged cords into the laptop, turned up the volume, and listened for a moment before muting the speaker. He glanced out the window, did a quick count, and grabbed the corresponding number of fiber-optic digital recorders.

He walked through the alley at a relaxed pace until he reached the first of the police cruisers. He checked his periphery and opened the back door. He placed one of the pen-cap-size devices under the passenger seat.

"Cops," he said, shaking his head.

Widow placed one recorder in each of the cruisers and returned to his car. He let the seat back, took a sip of espresso, checked the angle of the directional microphone, and turned up the volume on his laptop.

"All right, gentlemen, you're live in five, four, three..."

* * *

"This psycho is losing it," Reggie Karakas, a department lab tech, said.

"You think he's losing it, eh? What, could it be the coupla dozen tags we've handed out in the last two days? Or is there some other reason this psycho is losing it?" Pat asked.

"Maybe the guy with the missing fingers thinks different," a voice from behind him said.

Pat glared at Karakas, who immediately immersed himself in processing the scene, before he turned to face the source of the comment.

"Why are you here?"

"Because I can be," Detective Sergeant Nathan Davis replied. "And because it seems you and your partner are incapable of finding anything but a trail of bodies. Speaking of which, where is your better half?"

Pat ignored Davis and walked into the kitchen, rubbing his hand along the countertop.

"What are you doing?" Davis asked.

Pat continued until he got to the sink. He reached under and grabbed a bottle of bleach. He brushed past Davis and went back into the family room.

"Karakas, does this room look odd to you?"

Karakas shot Pat an incredulous look.

"You mean other than this guy?"

Pat shook his head. A frustrated sigh punctuated

his growing irritation as he sat down on the couch. "You can't see the TV. Damn recliner's in the way. Who the fuck has a La-Z-Boy between the TV and the couch?"

Pat got up and walked to the recliner. He thought for second and pushed it over. "No, Karakas, this psycho ain't losing it," he said, pointing to the bleached spot. "He's not losing a goddamn thing."

"He cut a man's fingers off; clearly he's not wrapped tight," Davis shouted from the kitchen.

Pat stared into the distance, a mixture of astonishment and exhaustion fixed to his face. Karakas stood and met his eyes, his gaze full of pity.

"Sir, it's most likely because the vic fought back. During the fight, I suppose he scratched his attacker," Karakas said.

As Davis *ahhed*, Pat rolled his eyes and lit a cigarette.

"No smoking on scene," Davis said.

Pat stalked outside, mumbling something about getting some air, and put his cell to his ear.

Davis watched him disappear and turned to Karakas.

"Have we got anything?"

"Sir, I can't speak for the others, but this is the third scene I've processed, and I haven't found a single thing."

"Fingerprints, hair, saliva, semen? You haven't found anything?"

Karakas began to wish he'd joined Pat outside.

Det. Sgt. Davis was getting on his nerves.

"Sir, this one is careful. He cut a man's fingers off because he may have had DNA under his nails. And as far as I know, he hasn't jacked off on any of his victims, so semen is a no."

* * *

Widow laughed aloud from his SUV. He was beginning to like this Arch Angel. The man was good, very good. Widow appreciated a man who took his work seriously.

He's got style; I'll give him that.

"But I fear you may be too clever by half, Mr. Angel," he mumbled to himself as he grabbed another laptop and punched a few keys.

The search program opened. He filled in some of the parameters using the information in the files Ted Allen had given him. When he reached CRIMINAL RECORD?, his hand hovered over Y for a second before he pushed N.

He completed all fifty queries. Some answers he knew as fact. Others, like Special Forces training, he assumed. The program would run for several hours, compiling a list of possible Angels. He pulled out a satellite phone and dialed.

"Yes, Mr. Drake," Ted answered.

"Expect a target in twenty-four hours."

"That soon? Mr. Drake, your value can't be overstated. I—"

Widow hung up before Ted could get further into his monologue. As it was, he wouldn't be surprised if Ted continued for several minutes before noticing he was alone on the phone.

Widow turned up the speaker and listened. Pat McConnell was gone, likely to meet his partner at another scene. Karakas and Det. Sgt. Davis were alone inside the apartment. Karakas must've been by himself because Widow could hear him complaining about Davis.

Widow smirked. He felt sorry for the lab tech. He adjusted the laser microphone, aiming it at the bedroom window. After a few seconds, he heard Det. Sgt. Davis talking to himself. Unless he'd lost his mind, Widow figured he was on the phone. He reached to unplug the microphone as another voice— one that did not belong—joined his recording.

"...another twelve. My, my, he's been a busy boy."

"Dammit, Ted, are you enjoying this?"

"Nate, don't forget who you're speaking to."

Apparently, Detective Sergeant Nathan Davis liked speakerphone—and was used to capitulating to Ted Allen.

"Of course, Ted. I just meant this is getting out of hand. The FBI is going to take over; I can just feel it. McConnell couldn't find his asshole with a flashlight."

Dumbass, Widow thought.

He wasn't the only one with that sentiment.

"Nate, the best asset of a good leader is recognizing what he has in his people."

"I don't follow."

"Of course you don't," Ted replied. "Just stay out of the way. I will have something for you tomorrow."

Only Davis and Widow heard his stammering reply. Ted had hung up. Widow closed the laptop lids harder than necessary, jerked the cords free, and tossed them to the floor.

He wasn't sure why he was angry. This development didn't change his job at all. He would still find the Angel. He'd still collect the remainder of his hefty sum for services rendered from Ted.

But will I put a bullet in his head after?

"That depends on what else I find out about Ted," he said.

Widow heard shuffling steps an instant before the barrel came through the window.

"Git out, douchebag."

Widow regarded the bald man with an eagle tattoo on his dome. He was in no mood to deal with the lower rungs of society.

"Go away."

"Don't tell me what to do. Get your ass out."

The skinhead cocked the revolver in affect. Widow fired the suppressed .45 sitting in his lap for *effect.* The bullets tore through the door frame, followed by the would-be robber's left leg. He would've collapsed if Widow hadn't grabbed his arm.

The man howled in pain. Widow slapped the gun out his hand and handcuffed him to the inside of the vehicle. He met the man's wild gaze with a sure smile.

"Let's go for a ride, shall we?"

Widow hit the accelerator, shooting the powerful SUV backward down the alley. Every scream and a sickening crunch, when he didn't quite clear a dumpster, brought him a little closer to his quarry's mindset.

I guess we all have a bit of Angel in us.

16

Rosie didn't drink much.

"Chile, you three drinks from yo' back an' five from fa'getting how you ended up there," her grandmother used to say.

Grandmama, you'd be proud. I had six, and my virtue is still intact.

The cab driver pulled up in front of Mama's flat. Rosie handed him a wad of cash and told him to keep the change. She looked up at the stairs, willed them to stop swaying, and took her first ginger steps upward.

With much more skill than the usual occasional drunk possessed, Rosie ascended the stairs, got her key into the lock on the first try, and tumbled into the house.

When she entered the kitchen, and saw her family for the first time since that morning, she uncharacteristically met them with a smile.

"Helloooo, everybody."

Marcus, a marijuana blunt in one hand, a cell phone in the other, waved. Mama had her back to her.

She was wearing her gold tracksuit, which could mean only one thing.

"Going to the boats, Mama? Good luck."

When Mama turned to face her, she eyed Rosie from head to toe. Surprise partly, disgust mostly.

"You like my new dress?" Rosie asked, spinning around to give her mother a good look at her Saks Fifth Avenue purchase.

"Hmph. I guess ho'in do pay." She turned to Marcus. "Baby, you gon' run me down to da boats?"

Rosie just smiled at Mama, humming "Moving On Up".

"Whatcha sassin' 'bout?"

Rosie twisted the cap from a bottle of artisan water and took a drink, finishing it. When she was done, she broke into song—full-throated homage to George and Weezy getting a deluxe apartment in the sky.

"Lil gurl, whatcha sanging 'bout?" Mama asked again, truly curious and undeniably angry.

"Mama, I'm moving. Got a new place downtown. It'll be ready this weekend," Rosie said, grabbing Mama's shoulders and shaking her.

Mama recoiled, slapping Rosie's hands away. She grabbed her purse off the table and pushed Marcus in the head.

"Boy, run me down to da boats."

Marcus got up and walked out, mussing Rosie's hair on the way. She wasn't sure if he'd heard a thing going on, or if he did, that he cared. Mama stood on her heels, rocking back and forth, glaring hard at

Rosie, who bore it with a smile.

"Ya still owe me on da rent."

Rosie reached into her purse. She tossed a few bills at Mama, who snatched the Benjamin Franklins from the air with admirable skill.

"Yous a ungrateful-azz lil helfa."

"Mama, be nice," Rosie said.

"Hmph, I won'cha gon' befo' Friday. I won'cha outta my house ta'morra."

Rosie didn't protest. She smiled and nodded.

"I love you, Mama," she said.

Because my grandmama taught me to love my enemies.

"Whateva. You jus' be quiet. Willie bin feelin' bad all day. He up in da bed sleepin'."

Mama shouldered past Rosie, stalking down the hallway, cursing to herself about the Lord giving her this ungrateful slut for a child and other niceties. Rosie had heard them all before, in some fashion or another. Tonight she was immune to the barbs.

Rosie sat down at the kitchen table and exhaled. The day seemed like an entire month jam-packed into twenty-four hours.

Given the keys to the story of a lifetime—not to mention an advance, threatened by a couple of police detectives, signed an eighteen-month lease on a brand new studio loft apartment downtown, splurged on herself for once, got a little tipsy, and got the pleasure of telling Mama to go jump. She was exhausted.

Rosie pulled herself from the seat, got another bottle of water, and headed upstairs. She *was* being quiet. Not because of Mama, *'cause forget Mama*, but so she didn't wake Willie.

Willie. I'll never have to see Willie again.

The thought was the topper for this day. It *could not* get any better. She took one look at the bathroom, considered the schizophrenic shower, and headed directly for her bedroom. She went inside, scanned it and laughed hysterically.

"This could fit inside my new bathroom."

Rosie stood in the mirror, admiring her curves in the dress. She sighed in satisfaction as she unzipped it. She kicked her shoes into the crawl space that doubled as her closet and hung the black sequin cocktail dress on the rack she'd bought at Walmart.

She was about to begin her nightly ritual of lotion and oils when a grave error occurred to her.

The chair, the damned chair.

She turned to the doorway. In it, Willie stood leaning against the door jamb, his foot on the *damned* chair. There was no cigarette, but both hands were full. In one, he held a beer.

"Ya hut my feelin' dis mo'ning, gurl, goin' wit dat white man. But then I see ya shakin' dem hips fo' daddy an' I know ya wan' somma dis."

Rosie hurled the bottle of lotion at him, the only thing close, and covered her bare breasts. The bottle glanced off Willie's arm as he advanced into her room.

"Gurl, taint gotta be like dat. Ya quit playin'. Ya

knew I bin standin' in da doe'way, while ya swingin' dis way an' dat. Come on nah."

Rosie screamed. She jumped from her bed and tried to go around him. Willie seized her waist. He pinned her arms to her chest, grinding himself against her backside. Willie licked her ear. Saliva, putrid and dank, dripped onto her shoulder.

"Hmmm, whatcha call me, baby?" he taunted.

"Aahhh! You sick sonuvabitch, let me—"

The rest of her words came out in a huff as she slammed into the wall. She collapsed on the bed, coughing. Whether it was the alcohol or the collision, Rosie was bereft of strength, and Willie knew it.

"Das righ', baby. Jus' calm down. Let ol' Sweet Dick give ya a lil sometin sometin."

Willie started toward the bed, removing his tattered robe. Rosie tried to suck in more air, tried to get up. Her lungs and body failed her.

"Come hur, baby," he said, snatching her by a handful of hair. "Do me like ya mama do."

She looked up, first at the thing he held, then with frenzied hatred into his licentious expression.

Damn you, Willie. Let's get to the beating now.

She spat right in his face. A spark of rage flashed behind his lustful gaze, and then, to her disgust, he wiped the spit from his cheek.

"Das righ', baby. Ya know hah Sweet Dick like it." He rubbed her saliva up and down his shaft.

He wrenched her head tighter and pulled her closer to his midsection. She shut her eyes and sealed her lips, gritting her teeth. She clawed at his naked body. As she anticipated, Willie yelled and reared back.

The blow never came.

When she opened her eyes, the overhead light had been turned off, or probably broken. The streetlights cast ghostly shadows all over her tiny room. At present, one of those shadows was guiding Willie forcefully toward her dresser. And Willie wasn't trying to fight back so much as fight *away*. Every attempted retreat was met with a violent redirection. Rosie sat motionless, mute, horrified.

Willie alternated between begging Rosie for help and threatening his unseen assailant, and when that didn't work, he bargained—offering weed, money, harder drugs, Mama, and Rosie, "cause dem bitches some freaks."

Willie's exposition ended in a final, furious attack, which culminated in him being driven to the floor face first. Rosie cringed when she heard the crack.

The lure of the macabre pulled her eyes to the bloodied mess that was Willie. He lay curled in the fetal position, or would have if his arm wasn't crooked to the side in an unnatural way. She didn't know if he was dead or alive.

"Cover yourself," the shadow said.

In the darkness, she couldn't tell whether he was watching her, but considering he'd demanded that she get dressed, she ignored normal decorum. Rosie got up and threw on a T-shirt and jeans. When she sat back on her bed, a black, shiny thing came out of the shadow, reflecting the dim street light.

"Shall I kill him?" the man asked.

"No," Rosie answered, surprising them both.

The man stood over Willie's broken body for a moment, contemplating. He holstered the gun. He pulled up her chair and sat. He propped his feet up on Willie, and reclined, most of his body obscured.

"Well, Rosalind, you wrote such a compelling piece, I think it's time for an exclusive."

[END OF PART II]

PART III:
17

"...I appreciate the offer. I'll be in touch. Bye," Mayor Carl Phillips said. "Asshole," he added after hanging up the phone.

"Who was that, sir?" Deputy Chris Watson asked.

The mayor didn't respond. Rather, he reached into a desk drawer and retrieved a bottle of antacid. He popped the top and downed a few swigs. He started to put the antacid back in the drawer, thought better of it, and placed it on top of his desk.

"That was Ted Allen. He was calling to offer support and to—and I quote—'help the city through this time of crisis'."

"And by help?"

Mayor Phillips grabbed the bottle of antacid and took another drink, muttering to himself all the while.

"He's coming for us, Chris. That's his idea of help: unemployment."

"Sir, we need to be preemptive. We can't just wait for him to ambush us."

"And how do you suggest we do that?"

"Call in some favors. Get some of his biography out there. Remind the people of this city why Ted Allen can't be trusted."

Mayor Phillips was incredulous. His mouth moved, but no words would come. He just stared at his second-in-command, mouth agape, like a mime. Eventually, he buried his face in his hands and groaned.

"We can't do anything about Ted Allen right now. You are aware we have a serial killer running rampant through my city, aren't you? If we were caught playing politics at a time like this…"

"Sir, we can't just sit idly by—"

"Enough," Mayor Phillips yelled. He stood over the desk and slammed his fist down on it. The bottle tipped over, and chalky white antacid puddled over paperwork. "We have a disaster, for Christ sakes!"

He lowered himself back into the chair. He picked up the antacid to take another drink and flung the empty bottle into the trash can in disgust. Shutting his eyes, he gripped the desk. After a moment white knuckles regained their color, bullish breathing returned to normal. He opened his eyes slowly, as one who falls asleep underneath the brightest afternoon sun, and regarded Chris Watson.

"Our number one priority, our only priority, is making sure this psychopath is stopped. We *should not, cannot* engage in political gamesmanship right now. What Ted Allen does, he does."

Mayor Phillips spoke in a measured tone, yet just below the surface, a cauldron of white-hot fury bubbled. The veil was thin enough that Deputy Watson could feel the heat. He wasn't so obtuse; the matter was closed.

"I had Detective McConnell picked up as you requested," Watson said, changing subjects.

The smile that crossed the mayor's face felt like a slap to Deputy Watson's.

"See him in on your way out."

Deputy Watson was nearly gone when a voice beckoned him.

"And Deputy, make sure your thoughts are on the business of *running* the city."

"Of course, Mr. Mayor," he said without stopping.

A few moments after the mayor's dejected subordinate left, a surly detective took his place.

"Patty," Mayor Phillips said, rising to embrace him. "I'll tell you what, son, you're the spitting image of your old man."

Pat returned the embrace, though with far less enthusiasm. He took the offered seat and immediately put a cigarette to his mouth.

"You know there's no smoking."

Pat fixed the mayor with a disbelieving, slightly irritated glare.

"But then again, I could be persuaded."

Pat took the hint and tossed the pack of Camels across the desk. Mayor Phillips didn't hesitate.

"Ahh. The wife would kill me if she knew," Mayor

Phillips said.

"I don't think you brought me here to share a smoke," Pat replied.

With the vigor of a former three-pack-a-day man, Mayor Phillips smoked the cigarette down to the butt and deposited it in a teacup.

"No, Patty, I want to hear about your case."

"Then why not talk to the chief? I got work to do. And this ain't it."

Mayor Phillips bore this response, unflinching. *What's old is new again.* "Brian's a good cop, got a good head on his shoulders or I wouldn't have made him chief. But, honestly, it's a lot like you and Detective Maguire."

"What of it?"

"When Brian and your old man were together all those years, we all knew. Brian did fine work, was a good cop. Your old man? He was *the* cop—there's a difference. And that's why I'm talking to you."

Mayor Phillips let the words hang, daring Pat to interject. Pat stood mute, stuffing another cigarette in his mouth.

"So, now that we're done with our little reach-around, are you going to do your mayor the courtesy?"

"I didn't vote for you," Pat said.

Mayor Phillips looked across the desk into the man's stoic face and burst out laughing. He laughed hard and long, until tears wet his cheeks and his sides hurt as he tried to fill his lungs with air.

"Screw you, McConnell," he said between hacks

and chortles.

Pat settled back, satisfied, and said, "We know what it's not. It's not a 'mommy didn't love me/daddy touched me', sick-ass sadist."

"You know this because...?"

"Well, the guy spent the better part of yesterday disposing of a few of them in a most malicious manner, but it was all to cover his tracks. He's not coming unhinged, not getting off on killing like they always do. Nope, he's not garden variety. He is, or was, a regular Joe."

The mayor considered this for a moment and shook his head. "No, no. This isn't your garbage man by day, killer by night. There's another angle here. What's your real theory, Patty?"

"I don't know yet. But I know this much: this shit isn't random. Random is messy; random leaves clues. These murders are planned to a T. There's a connection with all the vics; I just can't see it. Yet."

Mayor Phillips wanted the antacid again. This conversation was not easing his heartburn at all. Another cigarette would have to do. He was pacing now, smoke trailing him like steam from a locomotive.

While the mayor worked off calories, Pat glanced at his desk. A fax with HOMELAND SECURITY at the top caught his attention. He couldn't make out the face or affixed note, only the name: Widow Drake. Curiosity stretched his hand; the mayor's voice pulled it back.

"Patty, do you think it's one of us?"

"What, a cop? Nah, it's not a cop."

"You sure?" Mayor Phillips asked.

The skepticism in his voice should have roiled him, but Pat was tired, exhausted really.

"Nope, it's not a cop. Not saying a cop's not capable, but the deal is all wrong. When we go bad, the shit happens in our circle: our CIs, our suspects, our districts. Shit's too spread out, no steady stream from a cop's POV."

Mayor Phillips nodded as understanding dawned.

"You already checked," he said, as much to himself as to Pat.

Pat didn't reply. He retrieved his Camels from the mayor's desk and made his way to the door.

"If that's all..."

Mayor Phillips walked behind him and grasped him by the shoulders. Pat turned to scowl in the mayor's face, a protesting *what* already forming on his lips.

"A couple more things," the mayor said. "The lady who wrote the article yesterday has an interview on the midday news. You may want to tune in."

As Mayor Phillips watched the wheels turn—the furrowed brow, a clenched jaw that probably wouldn't leave Pat's countenance for several hours, if at all— he felt sorry for the man. Pat, like his father, was incapable of understanding the mechanisms of the real world—how they worked and, more importantly, how to work them. He would retire, or die, a decorated detective just like his father, with the talent to be much more.

The phones, cell and landline, and computer instant messenger beeping together in a bothersome melody reminded Mayor Phillips of *his* real world. *Well, maybe they know something I don't.*

"Your old man would be proud."

Pat crooked his head and said, "The old man was a hardass," and walked out.

"Yeah and you're a teddy bear," Mayor Phillips said to the empty room.

18

Water splashed on Rosie's forehead and ran down her back. De'borah, her stylist, worked the spray hose with all the skill of a four-year-old. She put copious mango-vanilla shampoo into her hand and slathered it on Rosie's head. Judging by her fingers, De'borah tore out as many hairs as she washed.

Rosie wasn't even there. Not really. Much of her was stuck back in that old, dingy "hot as hell in the summer, thank God it's the winter" bedroom—a place where she'd been almost raped, saved, horrified by the act of saving, and emptied by the conversation that followed.

Shortly after the man had left last night, Rosie had grabbed her cocktail dress and new shoes and stuffed whatever else could fit in her overnight bag. Most of her belongings stayed in the bedroom, with Willie.

Poor Willie. She couldn't understand her concern for her would-be rapist. Maybe it was the ferocity of the beating. Maybe she wasn't made for revenge. She'd glanced back at him before she left the room for the last time, light from the hallway illuminating the heap. *If* Willie survived, he would never be the same. Those shadows, the Angel, had left *no* part of Willie uninjured.

She ran into Mama on her way out, *because of course she would come home then.*

"Willie's hurt badly. You need to call nine-one-one," she'd said.

Rosie hadn't paused to see the scene unfold. The word *rape* had hovered on her lips for an instant, but then she'd thought, *Why bother?*

Rosie had been on the front steps when the first wails reached her ears. In some corner of her brain, Mama had to know that Rosie could not physically have done to Willie what he'd suffered. Still, Rosie knew she would be blamed. Never mind that Willie was nude inside her room. Mama would tell anybody who cared to listen that Rosie had lured sweet, caring Uncle Willie into her bedroom and attacked him.

Rosie had been almost to the cab when Mama, phone in hand, had ripped open the front door.

"Yous a dirty, filthy thang. Git back hur. Ya bitch. Ya slut. Ya ho. Git back hur."

"Bye, Mama," Rosie had said, without sorrow, with finality.

Rosie now looked in the mirror. She should've seen De'borah yanking her head, spreading beeswax on each dreadlock. Instead, the reflection showed her grandmother in her favorite old chair, a ball of yarn in her lap and two knitting needles in her hand.

You done got yo'self in a pickle, girl. Hee hee. Don'

you worry yo'self none, baby. The good Lord will see you a way.

"Grandmama," Rosie said.

"What?" De'borah asked.

"Nothing, I was talking to my grandmama."

"Oooookay," De'borah replied, mouthing that Rosie was crazy to her neighboring stylist, as if she wasn't standing in front of a mirror.

Way I figure, you got three mens after you," Grandmama said. *"You go with the one you think gon' love you and take good care o' ya'll chilluns. How you think I picked yo' granddaddy? I had three mens after me, and he was the ugly one. Hee hee. I gave yo' daddy, God rest his soul, this same talk, but 'spect he didn't listen to a word I said, seeing's how he picked that woman that 'came yo' momma. Lord help me, but if that woman ain't the most evilest thing since that devil learned howda talk.*

"Grandmama!" Rosie shouted.

De'borah ignored the latest outburst. She just yanked Rosie back into the chair.

"Owww."

I'm sorry, chile. I jus' get to ramblin'. Anyways, you pick the man that gon' care fo' you. Pick right, girl, or you gon' get yo' momma.

Rosie let herself be led to the dryer. The lid covered her head, and she closed her eyes, thankful for the temporary psychotic breakdown. She was feeling better, pulling more and more of herself back from *that* room.

Even through the constant drum of the hair dryer, she could hear the stylists and customers talking about the Angel.

"Girl, what's he doing that's really so bad?" one asked.

"I don't know. I think he crazy. I heard the man cut up this crack-head and then ate part of him. Swear to God, my auntie told me that," another countered.

"He didn't eat anybody. He's just out there getting rid of all the criminals. If you don't want the Angel visiting, don't break the law," another said.

The conversation went on. Everybody had an opinion, most were good, and the bad were shouted down in haste. The great irony of the discussion was that no one bothered to ask Rosie her thoughts. Most didn't know she was the one who broke the story, and the ones who did had no intention of letting facts possibly get in the way of their diatribes.

Rosie of yesterday would've jumped in immediately. Today, she sat under the dryer, thrilled with her anonymity, cracking under the weight of her knowledge.

Pick the right one, chile.

When the epiphany hit—a clear thought finally breaking through the haze of her consciousness—Rosie exalted. Loudly.

Everyone in the salon froze, then turned to her, irritation on their faces. Rosie didn't notice a single one of the reproachful gazes.

"De'borah, girl, I gotta run," she said, ripping the

salon cape off and tossing cash in one fluid motion.

Rosie snatched her coat from the rack and rushed outside, indifferent to the wind coursing through her not-yet-dry hair. She had her head down, rifling through her purse, when her phone rang. She checked the number: Ted Allen. She declined the call.

She cupped the phone and went back into her purse. When her fingers wrapped around the business card, she felt the sky open, heard angels singing. Her phone rang again, and she declined it without even looking. Rosie fell back against the wall, holding the card to her chest. She exhaled and pushed herself upright.

This is gonna be okay. I'm gonna be okay.

She started walking, almost strutting down the street. The sound of angels singing seemed to follow her every step. She didn't mind; Rosie was in a groove. The sun was shining; her hair, while wet, was luxurious; *and* she was on her way to salvation.

When she stopped at the corner, Rosie finally noticed the constant singing was coming from the horn of a black Maybach, which trailed her down the street. The serenading didn't subside until the back window slid down, revealing the hard, angry eyes of Ted Allen.

"I would hate to think our relationship has soured so quickly. I could swear I saw you ignore *my* call. Tell me it isn't so."

Rosie's mouth tried to form some sort of excuse.

"Get in."

She considered his eyes; the offer was non-negotiable. She looked down at the business card. She didn't have to get in. She could keep going.

"Ha ha ha," Rosie chuckled joylessly. *This is Ted Allen. Go where?*

She crumpled the business card, letting it fall to the ground before she settled in the backseat.

"He came to see me last night," Rosie blurted as the door closed behind her.

She said it fast, so she wouldn't have the strength to hold it back. Ted interlocked his hands and held them to his mouth. He breathed in deeply and stared straight ahead, though he wasn't looking at anything. He was in his own world. Rosie knew he'd let her in when and if it suited him. In the meantime, she had her own thoughts to deal with.

I picked. Please, God, help me. I picked.

19

Widow Drake pulled up in front of the bungalow. It was the fourteenth residence he'd visited since he'd woken. The search program had finished sometime in the middle of the night, and even after he'd run the names again, adding more parameters, he could only whittle the list down to twenty-four possible Angels.

Widow checked the current entry once more: Daryl Briggs, Corrections Officer. He'd already called Daryl's work number and found out he'd been on vacation for the last week and wouldn't be back for two more. He'd called Daryl's cell phone, and it went straight to voicemail. On the greeting there was a man, presumably Daryl, doing a very bad impression of Rupert Holmes' Piña Colada song and bragging about the babes in St. Thomas.

Widow exited the SUV and jumped the fence to the backyard. He did a cursory scan of the abutted house windows, checking for eagle-eyed retirees. Satisfied no one was peeping, he looked inside the sliding glass door.

Floor lock.

Widow took the long cushion from a decrepit chaise lounge on the back porch and placed it against one of the panes of the sliding glass door. He kicked the cushion, shattering the pane, and stepped into Daryl's kitchen.

At once, Widow was aware that the man singing about piña coladas was not on vacation. A half-eaten bowl of Lucky Charms or some other child's cereal had been left in the sink; a drip from the faucet had only filled the bowl a third of the way.

Widow tensed and pulled his Luger. The pistol Ted gave him was floating somewhere in the Mississippi River. He hadn't particularly trusted Ted before; after overhearing the phone call, he trusted him less.

The house was small, five rooms and a basement. Widow crept down the hallway. Two of the bedroom doors were open. The one at the end of the hall was closed.

He glanced in the first doorway. The space was bare, save a few hangers in the closet. As Widow approached the second doorway, he was overcome by an odor. He crinkled his nose and checked.

What. In. The!

The second bedroom was filled with soiled clothes and cat litter boxes. Inside one of the boxes, a cat was attempting unsuccessfully to find a place not covered with feces to do his business. After a minute, the cat gave up and used one of Daryl's shirts. Widow shook his head in disgust and holstered the gun.

"Scratch you, Daryl. You filthy, trifling—"

A muffled voice from a floor vent quieted him.

"You wanna die, huh. Is that it? You wanna die!"

Widow cocked his head and retrieved the Luger. A smile creased his face.

Then again, maybe not.

Widow was under strict orders to observe and report, not engage, and he reminded himself to *try* to follow orders. With that in mind, he opened the last bedroom door, checked it, and headed to the basement.

He descended the stairs quietly. The basement was dark and damp. The clothes, starting with a small basket in front of the washing machine and extending over the expanse of floor, swallowed any remaining noise of his nearly silent approach.

"Yah, yah."

Widow followed the yells to the only source of light. His back to the wall, he stood next to the doorway. His breath slowed; his skin tingled. He lowered to a crouch. At the end of a silent countdown, he whirled into the open space, index finger applying extra pressure to the trigger.

When he saw Daryl, he almost shot him on principle.

Daryl, all three hundred fifty unwashed pounds of him, sat drowning in potato chips. He wore a shirt that seemed only marginally cleaner than the one the cat had shit on, and a pair of boxers. Thick headphones covered his ears, his eyes fixed on an extremely large computer screen. An explosion from the online fantasy role-playing game lit up his face.

He was the wizard.

"Argh, I will confound ye," Daryl yelled into the microphone.

"You have got to be kidding me." Widow shook his head.

20

Pat stepped off the elevator into a tomb. Pencils scribbled nonsensically, keyboards clicked, coffee percolated into stained pots, and copy machines spit out hot sheets, but none of it registered with anyone. Uniformed officers walked up and down corridors with thousand-mile stares.

Inside the detective squad, the mood was no different. Files on every desk reached higher than the person's head buried behind them. A somber quiet had replaced heated case discussions and jovial baseball talk.

Pat navigated the malaise with a *hi* here, *how you doing?* there, and conversation nowhere. He got to his desk and fell into the rickety chair behind it. He could feel the faces, one by one, turning to him. Their eyes scrutinizing and questioning, all wondering how long Pat McConnell would be chasing the Arch Angel. How many bodies?

He wanted to yell, "Two days! I've been on it for two fucking days." He didn't. Not because it wasn't true, but because he too wondered.

"Norman, Lou been back?" he asked.

Bill Norman, a senior detective who Pat thought should've retired during the first Bush administration, gestured to Lou's empty desk.

"I can see that, nimrod," Pat countered. "I said *has he* been back?"

Norman cupped his ears, his face contorted in a "*huh?*"

"I said, where the fuck is Lou?" Pat yelled.

"Oh," Norman said. "How the hell should I know? He's your partner."

Pat gritted his teeth and balled his fists. He wanted to pummel the old detective. He kicked the bottom of his desk instead.

"He's on the fifth scene from yesterday," someone called. "Phone's on the charger. Said raise him on the radio if you need him."

Pat didn't know who'd spoken and didn't much care. He threw his hand up in a general thank you, shot a few daggers at the oblivious Norman, and sat back down at his desk. It was then that he first noticed his guest. The gaunt, silent man reclined in a chair, hidden behind the stack of files.

"Father? Father Brown."

When Pat spoke, the priest sat up, putting both elbows on the desk. He put his head in his hands and ran them through his mane. Pat was taken aback.

Father Brown's hair was thinning—at that very moment. Silver strands of his usually thick hair stuck to his moist hands as he pulled them away. Bags under his eyes drooped low, as did the wrinkles on his face. His nose was red, cheeks flushed, and his breath smelled like a winery. When he tried, and failed, to smile, Pat could see chalky white residue on his gums.

"Can I have a moment, Patrick?"

Pat didn't have a moment, but the desperation in the skeleton's voice made him reconsider.

He got up and led Father Brown to a conference room.

"Coffee?" he asked.

"Why, thank you. Yes, yes, that would be nice."

Pat filled a mug with hours-old coffee. Handing it to Father Brown, he sat on the table and regarded the priest as he sipped. Sunlight streamed through the window, doing the man no aesthetic favors.

"What can I do for you, Father? And if it's about me an' Maureen, I *really* don't have the time."

Father Brown glanced up from the coffee, confused as if he were trying to understand a foreign language.

"Who?"

"Who? Whaddya mean who? Maureen, my ex-wife. You counseled us."

Father Brown's face lit up in recognition, then darkened in anger. He slammed the mug down on the table. A coffee geyser shot into the air and splashed down, wetting both the priest and the detective.

"Your wife? Your wife! You think I'm here because of your failings as a husband? If only! Is that why you weren't taking my calls? You thought it was about your *wife*?"

Pat was momentarily stunned by the outburst. He turned from Father Brown, refilled the mug, and placed it back on the table in front of the priest. He exhaled and sat.

"Then what are you doing here?"

Father Brown leaned forward, so close that every breath he exhaled filled Pat's nose with the aroma of stale merlot. He clasped his hands over Pat's. Hard.

"You, you're the—what do they call it?—uh, yes, yes. You're the lead detective on the Arch Angel killer, right? I saw it in the paper."

"Yeah," Pat answered slowly.

"Tell me now. Are you close?"

Pat pulled his arms away and folded them to his chest. There was something off about the man. His eyes were wild, his voice anxious.

"You know I can't talk about an ongoing investigation. What's your interest?"

Father Brown exhaled, though it sounded more like a growl. He threw his hands up in exasperation.

"You tell me, Patrick McConnell. You tell me right now. Do you know who it is?"

Pat didn't answer. He craned his neck and glanced back through the window. Most of the squad suddenly had a pressing matter to attend to on their desks. Only Norman was too slow to react. His eyes were glued to the window, both hands cupped around his ears.

Fucking school girls.

He turned back to the priest.

"You don't know, do you? Oh, Lord in Heaven, you don't know. How can you not know yet?"

The question was more an accusation. Pat's patience with his *ex-wife's* priest was running thin.

"Look, Father, you need to relax. First, I'm not talking to you 'bout any case, much less this one. And second," Pat stopped suddenly. He crooked his head at Father Brown, and his eyes narrowed. "Hold up a goddamn minute. I've known you for what, ten, fifteen years? In all that time, you've never once been to my doorstep. Never once came in here lookin' like a damn wino asking 'bout my cases. Knowing what I know about the *winners* we've tagged at these crime scenes, I'm doubting very seriously they spent any time on *your* doorstep, so you got no personal stake. Why you really here, Father?"

Father Brown was immediately lucid, his eyes fixed on Pat. Pat matched his stare, probing intently. In the confessional, Father Brown was the master; in an interrogation room, suddenly under suspicion, he was ill-equipped.

"Patrick McConnell, how dare you take the Lord's name in vain?" he said, retreating to a place of power.

Pat shook his head. "No, sir," he said to himself. He continued murmuring with his head down for a bit longer and then froze. His eyes rose first, furious, followed by the rest of his head.

Father Brown shrank from the glare.

"I'll be damned. I'll be goddamned."

"Patrick."

"Stow that sanctimonious shit, Father. What do you know?"

Father Brown placed his hands on the table. He pushed himself upright in the chair and spoke with resolve.

"I know that my vows, given to God and His Church, are sacred."

"Father."

"I said to God," Father Brown shouted, the pain of sacrifice lacing every word.

The door opened, letting in a gush of cool air. Pat turned, ready to verbally push back the interruption.

"You gotta see this," Lou said.

"Not now, Lou," Pat seethed.

"Now, Kemosabe."

Pat looked from Lou to Father Brown and back again. Every fiber of his being wanted to berate or maybe even lay hands on the priest until a sentence beginning with the Angel's name jumped from his mouth.

That's the only reason he decided to go with Lou.

"Vows, Father? Fuck your vows," he said in the doorway, his back to the priest.

"I would think you of all people would understand the value of vows *and* the harm in breaking them," Father Brown replied quietly.

When Pat's entire body stiffened, Lou, while late to the party, instantly knew the name of the song playing. He took his enraged partner by the arm, pulled him the rest of the way out of the room, and closed the door. Pat grabbed the first uniform he saw and vented his frustration on him.

"You. Watch this goddamn door."

The uniformed officer, Adams, took one look inside the room, saw a shaken priest leaning on the table, and glared at him.

"Don't worry 'bout what happened; just watch the fucking door."

Lou led Pat to another conference room filled with detectives, white shirts, and the chief.

"What's up?" he asked.

"The girl is giving an interview."

"You brought me here 'cause she's giving an interview? I already knew, and I couldn't give a—"

"She says she met the Angel last night, says he has a message."

Pat glanced around the room. The expectant look on every face told him the same thing. He flopped down into an empty chair and waited for the commercial break to end. Half his mind was here, the other half with the priest in the upstairs conference room. Two people knew more about the Angel than the entire police force. More than him.

This shit is getting old real fast.

No matter. He resolved that the second this circus was over, he would get it out of *one* of them. "Father, you're gonna tell me something or I swear..."

"Shhhh. It's starting."

He flicked off the general direction of the comment and leaned his head back, grunting. In his inverted view, he saw Patrolman Adams walking and conversing with another man, a man who was not the priest Adams was supposed to be watching.

"Fuck!"

21

Rosie downed another glass of water. The lights were blazing, the makeup suffocating. She felt like she was sweating badly, but they'd dabbed so much powder on her face, she couldn't tell. The folded paper in her hand shook loud enough to be heard over the clamor inside the studio.

"Honey, it's going to be fine."

Rosie looked first at the hand on her knee, and then at the smiling face. If the smile was meant to be reassuring, it was unsuccessful. Rosie wanted to punch her right in those pearly whites. She wanted to rake out her eyes, step on her nose.

She knew damned well Marie Frazier couldn't care less about her. She could see it in her eyes, behind her eyes.

When Marie had woken up this morning, she'd had an interview with an "intrepid" reporter. Good story, gone tomorrow. Now she had, sitting in her chair, held together by string and duct tape, an *actual* conduit to the Arch Angel. This was anchor stuff, network stuff.

"It'll all be over soon."

"Thank you," Rosie replied, emotionless.

"Ten seconds, quiet on the set," the producer's assistant shouted.

Marie turned away from Rosie. She faced the camera and put on her *faker* smile.

"Welcome back. Today we have, exclusively at Channel 7, Rosalind Williams. For those of you who don't know, Ms. Williams was the first to break the story on the Arch Angel. A name, I believe, you came up with. Isn't that right, Ms. Williams?"

Rosie looked beyond the lights and set people. In all the stares intent upon her, she found the crystal blue eyes of Ted Allen. He stood quiet, nondescript, at the rear of the studio, his arms folded, leaning against a post. The puppeteer nodded once; the marionette performed.

"Yes, I and a few colleagues did."

"Fascinating, just fascinating. Can you tell us how you came by your information? How'd you piece it all together?"

Nice try, bitch.

"Now, Marie, you know my sources are confidential," Rosie said.

"Yes, and apparently they're very good ones. Now, Ms. Williams, how did it come to pass that you met the Arch Angel?"

"Not by my doing, I assure you," Rosie replied, wearing her best Marie fake smile.

Rosie paused and took another drink. The bracelet

she wore clinked against the glass. The paper fluttered on her lap.

Get it together, Rosie.

She adjusted herself in the chair, crossed her ankles, and placed her hands on top of the paper. In her periphery, she could see the producer gesturing, mouthing the words "dead air."

"Ms. Williams, can you tell us more? How did you meet him? Is it a him? How did you feel? Were you frightened, maybe excited? Perhaps in awe?"

Rosie whipped her head around. Tiny dreadlocks followed the rotation like fifty mini satellites. She glowered into the smiling face of Marie for an instant.

"*Awe* is not quite the word I would use. Yes, Marie, I was frightened. Wouldn't you be? I won't get into the particulars of how I met him; just suffice it to say, I did not initiate a meeting."

"Very well then. What can you tell us about him?"

"I can tell you," Rosie said, turning to the camera, "that he said he doesn't care at all about publicity. He wanted, no demanded that I bring his message to the people."

Marie crossed one leg over the other and leaned forward, her face solemn and full of concern. Rosie wanted to punch her again.

"His message, hmmm."

Marie took the obligatory glance into the camera, conveying the seriousness of what was to be revealed. Rosie felt sick. She also, to the audience, looked like she was looking into the camera. The lights were brighter, the set darker, but she found Ted. He'd heard the message already, offered and subsequently rescinded a few tweaks to it.

"Oh no, my dear, this is perfect," he'd finally said.

She didn't look to him for support, for none would be forthcoming. She wanted direction, orders. Ted, if nothing else, would give both in abundance. He smiled; she danced.

"What is his message, Ms. Williams?"

Rosie didn't acknowledge Marie. She turned toward the camera, toward Ted, unfolded the piece of paper in her lap, and began to read.

"My fellow citizens of humanity, I know you too are tired—tired of crime, tired of fear, tired of the scourge that would, if left unchecked, climb from the sewers and choke the life from you with its very stench. I say unchecked, my fellow citizens, because what have we? A justice system with a retention rate less than the average fast food restaurant. Streets that teem with miscreants who have no regard for you, your family, your future.

"I, fellow citizens, could no longer sit idly by, watching, the very soul of me torn asunder, as the wicked prospered, plundering the righteous. Twenty-seven of those souls I have consigned to Hell. Twenty-seven wicked who sold drugs, killed without compunction, raped our women, raped our children, got fat off *your* suffering. Imagine if the police would pursue villains with the same persistence as they hound me. Nevertheless, I can't be bothered by their shortsightedness, and I won't be led astray by their doggedness."

Rosie was at the end of the page. She took a breath, glancing around. The set was silent, save muted breathing and the whirring of machinery. Marie was statuesque—her mouth open, her hand frozen half way to it, holding a pen. Rosie caught Ted's eyes and his smile. He alone was gesturing to her about dead air. She knew the smile was genuine. The next part was his favorite.

"To the wicked, today I say, rest yourselves. Find the time to commune with whatever god you profess to believe in, if any god will have you. Today, fill your bellies with all the niceties you can bear; drink heartily. Fulfill every sinful vice your wretched minds can imagine. Say your goodbyes to the ones who love you, to whom you have no capacity to reciprocate.

"For when the sun rises tomorrow, know that a new day is upon us, a day of reckoning, a time of retribution. Tomorrow, God willing, Hell will be richer in bastard souls and we, the righteous, will be free to live in a cleaner world. In that, I will succeed or go to whatever eternity God deems necessary.

"Fear not, citizens, you righteous men, you brave women, you who toil in this vast wilderness we pretend is civilized society. By God's grace, I will not stop until the air you breathe is free from the stench of debauchery.

"To you, those who by oath are to protect and serve the very citizens I speak for, I pray that you do not endeavor to interfere. There are among you good and honest, hardworking men and women. Do not open yourselves to injury, your families to grief by attempting to defend the same abhorrence you are sworn to protect *us* from. I say to you as Paul wrote: 'For he is the minister of God to thee for good. But if thou do that which is evil, be afraid; for he beareth not the sword in vain: for he is the minister of God; a revenger to execute wrath upon him that doeth evil.' God bless you, fellow citizens. God bless us all."

Rosie put the paper in her lap. She turned to Marie and took a drink of water. Marie flinched as if she'd been shocked.

"Well, Ms. Williams, I don't know what to say. I wasn't expecting that, that's for sure. Really, it's alarming. I don't think our audience has quite recovered."

"I haven't either," Rosie said, an image of Willie's broken body flashing behind her eyes.

Marie just stared at Rosie, unblinking. Rosie decided to close the interview herself.

"Ms. Frazier, you asked me earlier about my impressions of the Angel. I would say he is very serious, very determined, and very skilled."

22

Sheets of rain washed against the windshield so hard the wipers strained to keep up with the onslaught. Pat pushed the cruiser faster.

"Hey, you wanna slow it up, buddy?" Lou asked, one hand on the dash, the other gripping the "oh shit" handle. "You're puckering my O-ring over here."

Pat responded by speeding up.

Lou let go of the dash for split second, intending to cross himself, but Pat whipped around a corner and hydroplaned into oncoming traffic. Lou mentally crossed his chest and sent a plea upward.

Pat skidded to a stop in front of Channel 7 News and jumped out with the car still running. Lou grabbed the keys, made a promise never to let Pat drive again, and followed his partner into the studio.

There were hundreds of people, some camped under a massive awning, others trapped in the sudden downpour—the utilitarian beneath umbrellas, the unprepared with purses, newspapers, or nothing. Competing news stations, radio, and every imaginable variant of media was here too, all congregated to get a minute with the Arch Angel's lady. If not a quote, a picture would do.

As Pat elbowed his way through the crowd, Lou tried to keep up, but his cries of "Police! Make way!" were drowned in the deluge.

"Forget this," he said.

Lou aborted his attempt to pierce the gallery. He returned to the cruiser, siren blaring, lights flashing, and loud speaker on.

This'll get their butts movin'.

He drove onto the sidewalk and into the parking lot. Most people moved, others had to *be* moved. A tap from the push bumper got their attention.

In a few minutes, he'd parked at the rear door of the studio. Pat was already walking toward the car with Rosie in cuffs. Lou couldn't tell if she was crying or if rain had streaked her face. Either way, she looked stricken. Ted Allen walked next to her, his face obscured by a planner, whispering in her ear the entire time.

Pat opened the door and put her in the backseat. He locked eyes with Ted, who wore a smug smirk, before he got into the cruiser. Lou turned to reverse out of the parking lot, took one look at Rosie's face, and decided to use the rearview mirror.

"Goddammit," Pat yelled, flinging a soaked box of Camels to the floor.

Lou leaned over and popped the glove box. He reached inside and retrieved a fresh pack from the carton Pat had put in there a couple of days before.

"Simmer down, Kemosabe, and get your head back in the fucking game."

Pat and Rosie looked at Lou the same way a kid looks at her soon-to-be-sainted grandmother when she overhears her saying *damn*.

Pat chuckled. "Yep, you're right. Fucking-A are you right."

He lit a dry cigarette and closed his eyes.

"You know who that was?" he asked Lou.

"Nah, couldn't see. I meant to ask you about that. Lawyer?"

"That, my friend, was Ted Allen. Seems Ms. Lois Lane here is the new favorite toy. You know what that means?"

"Yep, an army of lawyers will be waiting for us."

The car was quiet, Rosie's constant sniffles from the rear notwithstanding. Police headquarters was a few blocks away; time was almost up. Pat perked up, sat forward, and decided to get his head back in the fucking game.

"Go 'round back."

"For what?" Lou asked.

"Alien," Pat responded.

The rotund detective smiled wide. "'Round back it is."

23

Father Brown wasn't sure if it was the cassock, his age, or both, but he barely had to try before he'd convinced Patrolman Adams to escort him to the elevator. On the ride down, Adams had called Pat all types of colorful names. *Douchebag*, *prick*, and *assclown* seemed to be his favorites, because he kept repeating them.

The young officer had wanted to stay until a cab came, but he had to go back to work. He'd fished a fifty out of his pocket and handed it to the priest. Father Brown took the money, playfully chastised Adams about attending mass, and bid him goodbye.

Father Brown was up the street and perched on a stool inside a dive bar before the officer was back upstairs. When the first shot of whiskey went searing down his throat—because the dive bar didn't have merlot, and frankly it wasn't nearly as helpful as it had been forty-eight hours ago—he thought of Officer Adams.

He knew enough of Pat McConnell from his time with him and Maureen to see that on his best days he was irritable. Never violent with Maureen but... *She isn't six foot four, two hundred twenty pounds. Poor, poor boy.*

The priest took another shot of Jack and toasted to the future ass-whipping that had set him free.

"Another," he said.

The bartender came over, bottle in hand. She paused mid pour and considered the priest.

"Ain't you s'posed to give up drinking?"

The smirking priest said, "No, we don't have to give that up."

"Okay, honey, if you say so."

"Thank you. God bless."

"Hah, honey, look 'round. This ain't 'xactly Godly."

The next two shots hit home, and the priest stared at himself in the cracked bar mirror. It wasn't a man he saw but a contradiction.

"Principles and faith. It's all we have, right? If we let them go we have, what? A human race grounded in nothing and everything, with no real place to call home. Perhaps we have that already. But the dead."

The bartender stood aside as Father Brown talked to her, to himself, to nobody. She'd dealt with plenty of crying drunks in her time. Big, burly, tough-as-nails men who came to the bar and cried over shots of whiskey, but never a drunk priest.

S'pose it's all the same. A man's a man's a man.

"Honey," she said, refilling his shot and pouring one for herself, "I don't know what you talkin' 'bout, and not sure I wanna, but you gotta remember, this too shall pass."

"What?"

His look was incredulous, hers tranquil. She shrugged as if it were plain as day.

"Well, I don't know 'xactly what it means, just something old folks used to say when things got lean, which was a lot. This too shall pass. Think 'bout it. Makes sense. Good comes. Good goes. Bad comes. Bad goes. On and on. Then you die. 'Joy the good, wait out the bad."

Father Brown gazed into her brown eyes, past the garish mascara and liner, and saw genuine caring— no judgment, no pity, just honest to goodness care for her fellow man.

He fell face first onto the scarred bar. He cried softly because there was little strength left in him for a more demonstrative showing. The bartender rubbed the back of his neck. Her touch, fingers calloused from years of twisting bottle caps, soothed him, and sent tingles up and down his spine.

Father Brown wiped his eyes and nose, pulled his face off the bar, and took her hands in his. He brought them to his lips and held them there for a moment before he released them.

"It's *my* job to bring aid to the suffering, you know."

The bartender laughed, though it was more of a cackle—loud, almost obnoxious.

"Reverend, way I see it, we're in the same business."

Father Brown was about to correct her, but

thought better of it and downed his shot. She moved to refill it when he covered the glass.

"I think it's about time I go."

"In that?"

He followed her gesture to the window where it seemed all of Heaven had opened and was trying to wash away the filth from God's creation.

"Perhaps I should stay. Pour me another."

She started to pour, then stopped, staring intently.

"Coupla things, Rev. You ain't gettin' in a car, are ya? And you can pay for this, right? 'Cause we don't do credit 'round here, even for church folk."

"Will this do?" he asked.

She held the fifty up to the light, dotted it with a felt marker, and smiled.

"Yep, this'll do. Hell, you drink up, Rev."

Father Brown downed the shot and said, "I plan to. And call me Walter. I'm taking the day off."

"All right, Walter it is, and honey, you can call me anytime."

He smiled and stared at her as she left to take care of other customers. For just an instant, Father Brown felt whole again, able to enjoy a simple human emotion: happiness. Though when the rickety TV hanging over the bar showed footage of Pat leading Rosie from the studio in cuffs, he relinquished the feeling without a fight. He chose another, *simpler* emotion: despair.

And downed another shot.

24

Lou's chin rested on his chest. For Lou, he was snoring softly—the walls only vibrated a little. Pat pulled another cigarette from the box and discarded the empty pack. He nudged Lou's outstretched legs.

"What? I'm awake."

"It's time," Pat said.

Lou got up and blocked the door.

"You know we go in there an' we bring a shit storm down right on our heads."

"I know, buddy. You don't have to go in. I'm not asking you."

"Yeah, I didn't say that. Jus' puttin' all our cards on the table. We go in there, and we break the law. Hell, we're already breaking the law. You ever stop to think maybe *this* guy ain't worth it?"

Pat's face darkened, apart from the red aura cast by the fiery cherry at the end of his Camel.

"What. In. The. Fuck? Don't tell me you're becoming one of *those* people. Oh, the Angel; he's cleaning up the streets. Bless the Angel; he's doing God's work. I feel so much safer with the Angel around. Are you outta your mind?"

It was Lou's turn to glower. It was an expression he was unaccustomed to giving and one Pat was sure he'd never been on the receiving end of.

"Screw you, Pat McConnell. Don't you dare treat me like an asshole."

"Then stop acting like one. You asking me, is he worth it? I got no idea. What I do know? I know the psycho killed twenty-seven people and is gonna kill more. I know that girl is the best lead we got. Fuck the greater good, Lou. We do police work. And until somebody tells me different, jokers who kill twenty-seven people go down."

Lou fell back against the wall. He rubbed his eyes and sighed. He was frayed. Pat was too. The lone difference: Lou was yarn, and Pat was electrical wire. The scowl on Pat's face, rigid as if made of plaster, only began to soften when Lou threw up his hands. He pushed off the wall and started for the door.

"Let's go, then."

Pat stuck his arm in front of his partner and friend.

"You got misgivings 'bout the play. I go alone."

Lou turned to Pat, or rather over Pat, given that if someone were behind Lou in this particular instance, they wouldn't be able to see a person on the other side of him.

"We're partners, dickhead. We play it together. And just so we're clear, buddy boy, I don't cheer for murdering assholes. And screw you for implying."

After a momentary stare down, Pat relaxed. He

nodded, mimicking Lou's earlier eye rub and sigh.

"I know it, man. That was some other shit talking. I—"

"You absolutely, undeniably, unequivocally suck at apologizing," Lou interrupted. The glare disappeared from his face, and he stepped back. "So, before you hurt yourself, what say we go see what Lois Lane's got to say?"

"Fucking-A," Pat responded.

Lou opened the door. Pat walked in first and took a seat across from Rosie. Lou stood in the back, arms folded across his chest.

"Ms. Williams, are you comfortable?"

Rosie brought her head from the table and looked at him through dry eyes, empty from hours of spent tears. When they'd first brought her to the bowels of police headquarters, she was convinced Ted's lawyers would come in five minutes later and whisk her away.

As the minutes turned to an hour and the hours continued for what felt like forever, her brain—the distorted, evil, unfeeling thing that it was—kept replaying her time with the Angel. And when it decided to give her a break from that reel, it started on her relationship with Ted.

Her grandmother was silent. No messages from the hereafter, only the constant reminder that she was a pawn in a game she was ill-equipped to play.

"I'd like some water, please," she said, attempting to be defiant, succeeding only in being pitiful.

Lou got her a cup of water. Rosie picked it up to

find it only half full. She drank it anyway and asked for more.

"Now, let's get down to business," Pat said. "Nice job on TV today, by the way."

"Thanks."

Neither meant what they said.

"So, why don't you tell us when you met the Angel?"

Rosie glanced through the window into the dim hall. Pat followed her gaze and turned back to her, shaking his head.

"Ms. Williams, no one is coming for you. Not here. When you tell us what we need to know—and believe me, you will tell us—then I will let you go. Until then, we sit and admire each other's beauty, or we talk. Your choice."

Pat lit a cigarette and leaned back, crossing his feet atop the table. Rosie opened and closed her mouth several times, each instance punctuated by a longing glance at the darkened corridor.

"All righty then," he said, startling her. "We'll be back tomorrow. Maybe after a night, you'll be a bit more conversational."

Pat got up. Lou was already at the door. Rosie was frantic.

"What? You can't leave me in here."

Pat, at the door, checked his watch.

"Lady, it's almost eleven. We're off. See you tomorrow."

Rosie watched them leave. She heard the door lock

click. She rushed to the glass, trying to make out shapes, listening for voices in the hallway. Nothing.

This is a game. A show. They can't leave me here. What about my rights?

Then the time dinged inside her head like a church bell.

Oh my God, eleven o'clock.

She was a journalist, not a mathematician, but she was good enough to do simple arithmetic. Her legs no longer supported her. The floor rushed to meet her.

Rosie wanted to yell and scream, kick the table and bang the glass with the chair. Instead, she gave in. She quit the game of brinkmanship that was way above her pay grade.

"I'll tell you everything," she said.

The world stopped for a moment. Her breathing ceased, her body frozen, arms extended, reaching for help. After an interminable pause, the door opened. Pat and Lou got her off the ground and into a chair. Lou left and came back with a sandwich from Stellina's Pasta, her favorite, and a cup of coffee.

"I'm listening," Pat said.

Between chews, she told them about the night, starting with Willie and ending with the Angel. She described, in as much detail as she could, his height, weight, and build. She told them about his demeanor, how Rosie got the sense it was important to him that she understood what he was doing and why he was doing it. Then she mentioned the list.

"What list?" Pat asked.

The sounds of fast-moving shoes slamming against linoleum coming through the still-ajar door got everyone's attention.

"Uh, get a move on there, willya?" Lou said.

"What list?"

Rosie leaned forward and whispered. "He told me about everyone he plans to kill tomorrow. He wanted me to tell the world what they'd done, and after tomorrow, who they were. I wrote it down."

"Where is the list?"

"Don't say another word," Ted said, barging in with a team of lawyers and Chief James in tow.

"McConnell!" Chief James shouted.

"Where's the list?" Pat asked again, ignoring the newcomers. "Where's the goddamn list?"

Ted moved between them and slid his arm around Rosie's shoulders.

"Not another word."

Pat watched in frustration as Ted led Rosie out of the room. She glanced back once. She was sorry. She'd wanted to tell him, but in a few seconds, she was gone. Pat turned to Chief James, shoving one of Ted's lawyers out the way in the process.

"Shut the fuck up. Your client is that way," he said, pointing to the hallway. "Chief, do you know what you just did? The man gave her a list, a goddamn list."

"McConnell, *you* shut your mouth. Get out of here, and don't come back until I call you. You too, Maguire. Get the hell outta here."

"Lou had nothing to do with it; it was my play."

"Get out!"

25

Widow Drake stood inside the pitch-black foyer, silent and motionless. He was tired. He knew he probably should've saved the massive two-story for another day, but he was irritated that he'd made it through barely half the list of possible suspects.

He'd been a bit ambitious with his twenty-four-hour timeline, and though he could give a rat's ass about Ted Allen, he cared greatly about his reputation and his work. Widow was slightly relieved when he heard the News 7 broadcast on the radio. The Angel, gracious psychopath that he was, had given him an extra day.

So, ignoring his instincts in the dark of the night, he leaned against the inside of the front door, waiting for his eyes to adjust to the unnaturally dim house. Widow had a pair of night-vision goggles back at the car, but he detested seeing the world in greens and blacks unless it was absolutely necessary. In a short time, the scene took shape.

He proceeded through the foyer into the television room. Widow rubbed his hand along the couch cushions, checked the carpet and end tables.

He went to the kitchen next. The trashcan had a fresh, empty bag in it. The sink and towels were dry, the coffee pot unplugged.

Well, this is just great.

This suspect was supposed to be out of town, on leave from a security consulting firm, and unlike Daryl the super-gamer, he seemed to be.

Widow checked the rest of the lower level, finding it as vacant as the kitchen and television room. He trekked up the winding staircase to the second floor and went immediately to the master bedroom. The bed was made; the shower and sink were bone dry, the trashcan empty. Widow sat down on the bed.

There were several rooms left to check. He was tired. The house was clean. *Really* clean.

Reminds me of home, he thought.

In that instant, the truth of the statement washed over him. He was too damned tired. Lost his edge. He should've known the minute he walked inside.

Dammit. Everything in its place. Everything perfect. Meticulous.

Widow tensed. He left the bedroom and started back down the hall, this time slightly crouched, with his back against the wall. He checked the two guest bedrooms and found them as orderly and neat as the rest of the house.

Widow opened the door to the office. Light from the street shone through the not-quite-drawn curtains, splaying his shadow into the hallway. A different light got his attention, a blinking power button on the laptop on the desk. The computer was on, in sleep mode.

After a month?

He rolled the chair out of his way and started to push the power button with the Luger's barrel when the sliver of light coming through the window saved his life.

He dove out of the way just as two bullets tore through his reflection in the screen. Widow didn't even turn to find the gunman. He continued to the window with his head ducked.

Widow was in the air for a second or two before he crashed to the lawn in a pile of glass and window parts. The sudden pain radiating from his lower left leg told him something was wrong. A quick glance back to the second story told him he would deal with it later.

Hobbling, rolling, zigzagging, Widow made his way down the lawn with the occasional thump of a bullet in the dirt where the gunman thought his head would be.

Widow had been the man in the window before, watching his prey dance and whirl about, trying to avoid a bullet. It always ended the same way.

The first bullet lodged inside his already busted leg, the second sliced across his back. The leg couldn't support his weight any longer. He crawled, clawing at the wet grass, dragging the dead weight behind him.

His car was a mere hundred feet away, but it might

as well have been ten thousand at the pace he was going.

He was thankful for the respite from gunfire until he heard the front door open. The Angel's hard-soled shoes clicked with each step along the stone pathway.

Widow stopped his crawl and collapsed into the wet grass. The footsteps were only a few yards away now.

Que sera, sera.

The Angel stopped behind him. Widow waited for the instant where he would never hear again. Instead, he heard the Angel speak. A man of the Book would've noted that the Angel was quoting 1 Samuel 15:23: "Because thou hast rejected the word of the Lord, he hath also rejected thee from being king". A man like Widow had little use for holy books. He did, however, have use for a man who spoke when he should be shooting.

With a grace belying his condition, Widow flipped over and fired his Luger. His aim was true, and the Angel stumbled backward several feet before falling in a heap.

Widow looked around to the neighboring houses. Lights were coming on, with panic jumping from house to house like wildfire. Unlike the Angel's gun, Widow's specially built .357 Luger wasn't suppressed.

Widow forwent the crawl and stood up, balancing on his one good leg. He looked back at the prone Angel and grimaced. He really should finish him. He should hop over to him and put a few in his head.

Two things stopped him: One, he took his job seriously. His contract was not a hit. It wasn't supposed to get him shot either, but those were the perils.

Second, and more importantly, Widow knew what a person looked like when they got shot, and what Kevlar *sounded* like when it got shot.

"If we meet again, Angel," Widow yelled, hopping to his car as the Angel came to, hacking and coughing.

A few minutes later he was driving with his good leg, tying a tourniquet on the other, and dialing Ted Allen. Ted listened with great interest as Widow reported the successful end to his investigation into the Angel's identity.

Then Widow hardly paid attention to Ted's fanciful ramblings.

"Him. My, my. I'll get someone on him immediately," Ted said, with barely concealed zeal.

"Then our business is at an end," Widow said. "I expect the remainder of my fee within the hour."

Ted didn't answer for a while.

Widow was a patient man, but Ted was trying him, again.

"You'll have it in an hour. But since I have you, I may have another job for you."

"Another job? What is it?"

"I haven't quite worked out the details. Tomorrow?"

"That'll be fine, tomorrow evening."

"Good, I'll be in touch."

26

After leaving police headquarters, Pat found himself back in the old neighborhood. Reclining on the hood of his car, he shot imaginary bullets through cigarette-smoke Os into the night. He breathed in deeply, taking in the smells of his childhood digs, a real neighborhood where kids played on jungle gyms and swings instead of whatever new video game system was out. Where parents and grandparents all still lived close, and got together every few weeks whenever the old man decided to break out the barbecue grill.

A place where families were born, made a life, and died in the same house for generations—people setting down real roots, not transient renters who came and went with the seasons.

The Smiths lived up the street. The Jacoby family stayed two blocks over. The Fosters, Maureen's family, were on the outskirts of the neighborhood, the six blocks where the old racial lines had blurred and black and white families coexisted together.

In the center of it all, as in any real neighborhood, was the church. Theirs was St. John's. Pat hated going to church like any self-respecting rebel. His beef wasn't with God, but rather with what he saw as inane rules and regulations.

During the Maureen years, on the rare Sunday when the job hadn't taken him away, he'd attended mass with his wife. It was obligatory, but he did it with a smile, because that's what he was supposed to do.

Is this what you're saving, Angel? The neighborhood?

From the moment he'd walked into the junkyard a few days ago to find yet another crime done by criminals *to* criminals, the question had fluttered just behind his eyes. His argument with Lou had brought it to the forefront.

Why the fuck am I working so damned hard at chasing a guy taking out the trash?

The answer, of course, was obvious. *Because he's breaking the damned law.*

Pat knew that was the reason; he also knew that *wasn't* the why.

"Why? Why? 'Cause I don't get to, you fucking prick. I gotta put cuffs on every degenerate asshole I come across. That's fucking why. 'Cause I can't decide who lives or dies. I can't play God, and I'll be damned if you get to."

Pat flicked his cigarette into the night, its embers a furious and violent red.

Then his phone rang.

***

Pat drove slowly. Uncharacteristically slowly. He wasn't nervous; he was wary. Being beckoned at this hour to the seat of power was at the least unusual, as in this was the first time. Pat circled around through Forest Park a few times to collect his thoughts.

When he pulled up to the mansion, after being stopped by a few police cruisers, he noticed he wasn't the only visitor. He mashed his cigarette into the overflowing ashtray and got out of his comparatively understated car. The front door opened as he approached.

"Patty, thank you for coming."

"No problem, Mr. Mayor," he said, grasping the outstretched hand.

It all felt wrong. There was something off about Mayor Carl Phillips.

He seemed less like the mayor he was at City Hall.

The two walked through the house, Mayor Phillips's arm around Pat.

"Heard you had a bit of excitement earlier."

Pat didn't respond because at present, his eyes were glued to the black and white photographs lining each side of the hallway. Some were candid family shots, the kind taken in the backyard. Several others showed the mayor's time on the police force, some of which included Pat's father.

"Really, Patty, Alien?" Mayor Phillips said between guffaws. "Boy, I would've loved to see the look on Brian's face. That's the kinda thing your old man and him woulda pulled."

Pat looked into the mayor's face and reciprocated the smile. By the time they reached the parlor, he'd dismissed his earlier misgivings about Mayor Phillips.

The instant they stepped into the room, the temperature *and* the mood changed. The loose casualness fell from Mayor Phillips shoulders. His back straightened, and the smile he wore, while remaining the same, also looked different.

It's the eyes. He ain't smiling with his eyes.

The room was cold, frigid in fact, and in stark contrast to the warm ambiance a parlor—with its large, comfortable-looking leather couches; oak desk; faux gas lamps; fireplace; and thick, foot-massaging carpet—should've engendered.

The man who was already present there, sipping on a glass of brandy, added to the unwelcome feeling.

"Ah, Detective. I'm glad you decided to accept our offer."

Our offer?

Pat froze in his tracks, eyes darting back and forth between the two men in disbelief.

"Now, Patty, I know this is a bit awkward, but hear him out."

"Nah, awkward is when you're at a buddy's house for dinner and he overhears you calling his wife a cunt. That's awkward. This? I don't know what the hell this is."

"An opportunity, Detective. Now sit," Ted Allen said.

The mayor was already making his way to his seat. Pat shook his head and flopped down on the opposite side of the couch.

"Patty, something to drink?"

Pat caught the beer Mayor Phillips tossed him and popped the top. He drank without comment, and Mayor Phillips didn't see one forthcoming.

"Okay, Ted, tell him what you told me."

"Detective, we've had our differences, but in the interest of the public good, I feel compelled to share this with you."

Pat ground his teeth and wished for a cigarette. Ted Allen had talent; he could say a thousand words *without* saying a damn thing.

"I know who the Angel is."

Pat stopped grinding his teeth.

"How do *you* know?"

"My budget is bigger. My resources better."

"If that's true, why the hell you tellin' me? Why not the PD or the paper?"

Ted glanced at the mayor, and some unsaid exchange occurred between the two.

"Patty, he's telling you because I asked him to."

"What Carl means to say is this is a delicate situation."

"Really? And how do you figure that?"

"Because, Detective, unlike you, I see the forest through the trees. Do you know that right now, the Angel is the most popular St. Louisan?"

Pat had no comment. Partly because he was so sick of people admiring this psycho, but mostly because *I don't give a rat's ass!*

"Of course you don't, and you wouldn't care if you did. But you should. This man is the second coming."

"He's a murderer."

Ted laughed. The mayor grimaced.

"You're not that stupid. You can't be. This man single-handedly has every crazed killer, sick rapist, and lowly drug dealer in the city cowering. He's killed, yes. But you know as well as I do that people don't care how the trash is taken out so long as it is. Hell, I bet if our Mr. Angel wanted to run for mayor, he'd win. What about that, Carl? Which of you has the higher approval rating?"

For just an instant, the old police captain showed himself under the mayor's veneer. His chest heaved, and thick veins popped out of his neck. As quickly as the fire ignited, it cooled. Mayor Phillips regained his composure and nodded, neither in agreement or opposition.

The smile never left Ted's face.

"The point of all this is that even *you* undoubtedly realize it's only a matter of time before we have copycat Angels running around exacting their own brand of justice. And that will not do. He's good. He's fair. He's right. They won't be. A copy of a copy and all that... It's just bad for business."

"He's right? He's fair? What the hell's going on here?" Pat shook his head.

"What's going on here is the real world. This is how real business is conducted—by men in the know deciding how much those who are not need to know. This is how difference is made. You don't honestly think you're making a *genuine* difference? Cops and robbers. You can't be that dense."

"Ted, please," Mayor Phillips interjected. "The Angel, remember him."

Pat was angry but oddly restrained. Under normal circumstances, Ted's little dig would've sent him over the edge, but these weren't normal circumstances. He knew he was in the middle of something rotten and, at least for the moment, was more interested in finding the source of the rot than in thrashing Ted Allen.

"Look, assclown, you can take your business and shove it," Pat said. "You're an idiot with delusions of grandeur, but if you know who the Angel is, I'm listening. If not, I know my way out. Either way, stop wasting my motherfucking time."

"You're half right," Ted replied through a wide smile. "But in this instance, you are correct. Time is a luxury we don't have, and one I wouldn't waste on you if we did."

Motherfucker! How long can this dickhead talk about nothing?

"As I said before, this is a delicate situation, one

that requires a scalpel."

"And?"

"And," Carl said as he shot a glance to Ted, "that means we can't have a trial. We're not going to martyr the man. We're going to disappear him."

Pat laughed humorlessly. He ignored his previous personal pledge to respect the mayor's home. He was tired, he didn't play politics, and he was sick of them both. He reached into his pocket and pulled out a cigarette. He lit it and took a long drag, fixing a defiant look squarely on Mayor Phillips, and then turned to the man running the show in the mayor's parlor.

"Ted, go fuck yourself."

"Detective, please. He didn't say kill the man. As if you could. He said disappear him. You are to lead a team into his hideout and apprehend, not kill, the Angel. Once you have done so, there are avenues we will avail ourselves of to rid us of the Angel."

"Don't let the law get in the way of justice, eh, Ted?"

"You would know better than I, Detective."

"Gentlemen," Mayor Phillips said.

Pat and Ted both shot him a sidelong glance, as if they'd forgotten he was there and were extremely unhappy to be reminded.

"Think about it, Patty. Can you imagine the trial? This guy is a mass-murdering terrorist, but what happens when his lawyer starts in on his so-called victims? The jury's going to convict a man who's done nothing but get rid of our worst?"

Pat started to answer, something smart-ass composed of a few four-letter words littered among a response about law and order. But his mouth opened and then shut. He was angry, not an idiot. He'd seen what happened to solid cases with *bad* defendants when a good lawyer started talking. He couldn't imagine what the Angel trial would look like.

"Maybe they do, maybe they don't," Carl said. "You willing to risk it?"

"So we disappear him," Pat conceded. "The shit's already out; the story is already rolling. You think people are just gonna leave it?"

"People are fickle. The narrative doesn't drive the story, bodies do. The average citizen is no more concerned with the ethical and moral question of the Angel than you are with the Dow. Flashing lights, Detective. No more Angel, no more bodies. The story goes away in a few weeks."

Pat looked back and forth between Carl and Ted. He knew Ted was playing a game, playing him. What he didn't know was where Carl, a man he thought of as a friend and mentor, now sat. He was missing something—a big-ass flashing sign telling him what was truly going on. He couldn't see it, yet. He nodded knowingly and scratched the scruff on his chin. He had to admit, though Ted was a sleazy degenerate, he was right about the flashing lights.

"Fair enough. So, who is it and where do I find him?"

Ted stood and walked to the buffet. He refilled his glass and swirled the contents with his back to them. He stared at the wall, taking sips of the brandy. He was milking the moment of the big reveal.

"His name is Widow Drake," he said, without turning.

No, it's not, Pat thought, a millisecond from uttering it aloud. He couldn't remember where he knew the name from, but he knew Ted was wrong. *Wrong or lying.*

"Who is Widow Drake, and why are you so sure he's the Angel?" Pat asked.

"He's an assassin. He has more than two dozen bodies attached to him in half a dozen countries on at least three continents, not including this mess in St. Louis. He's extremely skilled, extremely dangerous, and, apparently, extremely unhinged," Ted answered quickly.

"You seem to know a lot about him," Pat replied just as quickly.

"As I said before, better resources."

"I checked his information," Mayor Phillips interrupted. "He's right."

"Let me see it."

"We don't have time. The Angel, or rather Mr. Drake, gave us a single-day reprieve. That day is nearly gone, Detective. You can either spend the next several hours going over information people much smarter than you have compiled and miss him, or you can trust us and be a hero. That, I believe, is *your* choice."

"Widow Drake. Eyes on the prize, Patty," Mayor Phillips said.

Pat wasn't about to let it go, but the mayor's words wormed their way through his anger and nested in his logic center.

Goddammit.

Pat knew Ted was playing him, but when he heard the mayor say the name, it finally dawned on him why the name was familiar *and* on which side of the fence Mayor Carl Phillips sat.

"You're right," Pat said. "Mr. Mayor, Carl, are you certain Widow Drake is the Angel?"

Mayor Phillips stood, meeting Pat man to man. He nodded and said *yes*, without breaking eye contact, without stuttering or slouching. He continued to speak, something about why he was so certain, but Pat didn't hear any of it. Once he'd said yes, nothing else he said mattered.

"All right, if you say it's him, good enough for me. Where is he? I got a few guys I can pull in."

"Hah, you mean your jolly Mr. Maguire? I think not," Ted countered.

"You little..."

"Gentlemen," Mayor Phillips shouted. Both men were shocked into silence, noticing the strain in his voice. Ted had to suppress a smile.

"Patty, I know you trust your people, and I'm sure they deserve it, but *I* trust you. This can't go wrong. I need you to handle it."

Pat looked down at the outstretched hand and up to the mayor's face, full of sincerity.

He almost believed it.

"Off the books," he said, grasping the mayor's hand.

"Off the books," Mayor Phillips replied, nodding.

"Everything you need is in here," Ted said, handing Pat a package, "including the contact for the team. They'll be expecting your call."

Pat took it and turned away, heading toward the door. He paused as Mayor Phillips gave him the obligatory "good luck" and "be careful."

"What about the list?" Pat asked, pausing in the doorway.

"What list?" Mayor Phillips asked.

Pat didn't so much as look at the mayor. His eyes were fixed exclusively on Ted Allen.

"There is no list," Ted said.

"What list?" Mayor Phillips asked again.

"Oh, okay. I must've heard wrong," Pat said.

Pat and Ted continued their stare down for a moment before Pat turned on his heels. Mayor Phillips buried his face in his hands once Pat left the room. The polish was cracking. His hand shook as he reached for his drink. Ted was supremely amused.

"Carl, you know I'm right. It has to be this way. If you didn't believe it, we wouldn't be here. I'm here to help."

"Don't bullshit me, Ted. If for a second you thought you'd be better served letting this play out in public, you wouldn't hesitate. You're here to help yourself."

"One hand washes the other, Carl. One hand," Ted replied.

"You're an asshole, Ted Allen."

"No, my friend, I am *the* asshole."

27

Detective Sergeant Nathan Davis sat in the rear seat of the blacked-out SUV, the first in a convoy of identical triplets. Around him, men in various stages of readiness grunted and farted. The two men stuffed in the back on either side of him were currently playing a rather lascivious version of marry-kill-bang with the ladies from *The Golden Girls*.

"Come on, man. That's just gross. Sophia must be crusty dry," one said.

"Says you. Pussy's like fine wine; just gets better with age," the other replied.

Nate wanted to throw up, roll his eyes, or tell them Estelle Getty, the actress who played Sophia Petrillo, was actually the second youngest of the "Girls". But instead, he laughed when one of the men—call sign Mongo—clapped him on the back, smearing a thick line of eye black onto Nate's shirt.

Nate suffered such indignities gladly, if perhaps a bit grudgingly. *The price of club membership*, Ted called it. They were men and women unknown to most St. Louisans, but who shaped the lives of everyday people nonetheless. He wanted to believe he was a member of the club, because a seat at the table of movers and shakers was what Nate craved above all else.

But he wasn't really one of them. He was just *among* them from time to time. Being Ted's cousin wasn't enough to grant him party, especially since that little genetic fact was a closely held secret, one conceived and fostered by Ted when Nate had moved to St. Louis several years ago. And while making detective sergeant was an impressive feat (achieved in no small part because of Ted's backdoor deals), Nate didn't possess the necessary cachet, lacked the signature bust, to move up much past that on his own.

"Do what I tell you, live smart, and I will make you chief of police," Ted had once told him.

It's my time, Nate thought, smiling to himself despite the smell and company.

The convoy was nearing the last position the tail Ted had put on the Angel had communicated. The tail should've given a more detailed report, but all Nate had received was a general location. That was troubling, but nothing would keep him from his glory.

"Up on the right," he said into the radio.

***

Pat's mind was so filled with scenarios and theories, he was getting a headache. He'd flipped through the dossier in the mayor's driveway. All the relevant info was inside: Widow Drake's aliases, likely locations, and the contact for Ted's team.

That was a call he had no intention of making.

And you know that, dontcha, Carl? You duplicitous cocksucker!

He'd toyed with the idea of calling Lou anyway but decided against it. With the whole Alien fiasco, Lou had gone as far to the blurry side as Pat felt comfortable leading him. Carl, his father's old friend and boss, who was apparently not to be trusted, was right about Lou. He was a good cop, but dancing with the devil always left a mark on you. Lou had none, Pat had many.

What's one more?

So, Pat sat alone in his car outside the Best Rate Motel, chasing down the only real lead he'd gotten since the Angel bullshit started.

Parked across the street, he stared through binoculars at Widow Drake's motel room. Television lights flickered through drawn curtains. Other than the flash from whatever infomercial was playing, the room was dark and absent of any movement.

"Fuck it," Pat said.

He tossed the binoculars on the seat, grabbed his vest, and started across the street. He walked through the gravel lot with his hands up.

"Drake. Widow Drake," he yelled.

Most of the Best Rate's business was done under darkened skies, by people for whom conversations with the law were anathema. As the Kevlar-wearing cop walked slowly along the decayed asphalt, screaming at the top of his lungs, rooms on either side of him in the U-shaped shithole were suddenly alive with activity. Curtains drew tighter, lights turned off. A few doors flew open and people in various stages of undress sprang from them as though SWAT, the FBI, and Interpol were hot on their heels. Cars, previously still, abruptly came to life and rumbled away, leaving acrid clouds of smoke and skid marks.

Normally, the exodus would've amused Pat. Right now, however, his attention was solely on the motel room in the center of the short side of the U.

He didn't know how much of the Widow Drake file was accurate, if any of it was, but finding out it was all true right after a bullet exited the back of his head was at the bottom of his list of "Things I just gotta get done tonight".

"Widow Drake. I just want to talk. I'm alone. Detective Pat McConnell," he yelled.

As he closed in on the room, there was still no answer or movement. Pat cursed. This was his play. One option, and no way to alter it once he'd committed.

Fuck me, I'm gonna get shot.

***

At the rear of a large parking lot, shadowed by a giant, abandoned-looking textile factory, two of the SUVs came to a halt—as did the juvenile, fun-loving attitude of their inhabitants. Almost before the trucks came to a full stop, all of the mercenaries exited. Though he couldn't see black figures through black glass under dark skies, Nate assumed the men in the other SUV moved in kind.

With all the grace of the amateur he was, he jumped from his seat. He flung open the door, and his hard-soled shoes clacked against the ground as he hurried to join the group. He alone made more noise than the rest of them combined. His intrusion was not welcomed.

The group—twelve, he thought but couldn't be totally sure—stood in a circle surrounding one man, call sign Buzzkill. He was giving marching orders.

Almost before Nate noticed, the group was light five men. Then, at some unseen, nonverbal signal, the rest of the men, clad in black—even the skin of the darker ones smeared in unreflective goo—faded into the night, leaving only Mongo and Buzzkill. Still, nothing had been said to Nate.

"Where do I go?" he asked.

Buzzkill didn't even look at him. Mongo turned, his teeth bright yellow against the black.

"Hah. Why don't you sit this one out, pretty boy? We got this," he said, just above a whisper.

"Hold on just a goddamn minute," Nate started.

Buzzkill pounced. He swept Nate's legs from under him. The detective sergeant hadn't yet comprehended what was happening when Buzzkill drove his knee into his chest and pressed a silenced Glock 9mm into his forehead. Buzzkill leaned in close, adding excruciating pressure.

"Shut your mouth. You are along for the ride, nothing else. The big man has his reasons. That's fine, but if you endanger my men again, I will personally put a bullet between your eyes and tell Mr. Allen the Angel shot you. Is that in any way unclear?"

The question didn't need an answer. As soon as Buzzkill moved, Nate slithered along the ground until his back was against one of the SUVs. He reached up and grabbed the handle, never taking his eyes off Buzzkill's weapon, and slid into the SUV, chased by quiet chuckles from Mongo.

He sat inside, wiped sweat from his brow, and tried, with little success, to slow the quivering of his hands.

After a moment he glanced around and spied a decrepit soul staggering over from the street. Nate almost opened the door to shoo the junkie away, but his encounter with Buzzkill convinced him to keep quiet.

Besides, just a junkie asshole. And a woman at that.

Nate smirked in hollow superiority and settled back in the seat. That served to calm him considerably, save his heart, which was still beating too fast.

Though he couldn't see any of them, Nate listened to the progress of the men on the radio. He couldn't hear much beyond the constant stream of whispering.

He turned his radio up as high as it would go and still could only pick up the occasional word.

He leaned against the headrest and rubbed his bruised chest, thinking about his bruised ego. He hated them, especially the only two he knew by name, but he needed them to be successful.

But, accidents happen.

"Maybe I'll be telling a story about him getting *you*," Nate murmured, reveling in a murder fantasy that he knew, even as he uttered it, he would never commit.

Nevertheless, it made him feel better. He stared intently, with renewed vigor, at the complex, listening again to the indiscernible grunts and words that apparently served as signals in Buzzkill's group.

His concentration was so complete that when the rap came on the window next to his head, Nate screamed—not a primal, guttural roar, but a wail more appropriate for a smaller, fairer creature.

The junkie woman outside, wearing a coat much too large for her skeletal frame, with ropes of matted, filthy blondish hair swinging across her face as her body shivered from a chilly breeze *and* addiction, parted her lips, exposing a smile of rotting and missing teeth.

"Get out of here now," he said in a fierce, low voice.

Nate let the window all the way down and stuck his face and gun out of it.

"Yo' friend said ta give dis ta ya," the woman said.

She seemed completely unaware or simply didn't

care about the pistol pointed at her face. She was Sandy, the former Emily, and guns were nothing new to her.

Three nights ago when, from her hidden enclave, she'd seen Juicy and several others for whom she'd plied her wares killed, in addition to being chased down and questioned by *stinkin' cops,* she'd decided to leave the 'row and get clean.

Her resolve had lasted less than forty-eight hours.

Now, having been given a promise of snap—a big bag chock full of soapy deliciousness—Sandy stood in front of the man she'd made for a cop the instant she saw him, to deliver a gift.

She handed Nate the phone. He took it gingerly, as if disease would jump off onto his skin. Sandy stifled a chuckle and made to leave.

"Don't you move an inch," Nate said.

Sandy stayed where she was. The cop's attitude wasn't all that unexpected, or especially frightening. She figured she could get away from him in a heartbeat if need be, so she complied.

The flip phone vibrated.

Nate dropped it to the floorboard. He retrieved it to a chorus of giggles from Sandy, breathing deep and wringing his hands.

He opened the phone and put it to his face.

***

Pat was on the sidewalk now. Just a few feet from

Widow Drake's motel room door. He took a deep breath and looked up—in habit more than faith, because he'd seen too much to believe in an active God—and crossed the sidewalk.

"Look," he said, speaking in a normal tone, "don't be an ass. If you were gonna shoot me, you could've done it already. If you let me walk all the way across this god forsaken lot yelling like a jackass just to shoot me now, I'm gonna be pissed."

He hit the door. When it swung open, Pat fully expected the glimpse into the dingy room to be the last thing he ever saw.

As it was, the cheap door slammed into the wall and recoiled back at him. He held it open and retrieved his sidearm.

Pat flipped on the lights and clicked off the television. The room was empty and clean. Aside from the smell of a recent fire, it was probably the cleanest room in the Best Rate.

He quickly checked the dresser drawers and under the mattress. Empty as expected. He went into the bathroom. Inside the tub, a metal pot was filled with papers, a couple of water bottles, pill containers, surgical supplies, used bandages, and what looked to be apple cores.

All soaking wet. Everything burned to a crisp.

Pat picked up the pot and threw it against the wall. Pieces of wet char and cheap tile littered the room.

"Come on. Give me a break. Just one fucking break."

The room phone rang.

Pat almost shot it.

***

"Detective Sergeant Nathan Davis. I admit, I'm surprised. Though the more I think about it, I should've guessed that the man I found at my house worked for your cousin. Ted Allen knows, more than most, that I shall reward his eagerness."

Nate stuttered and stammered, unable to form a coherent sentence of denial. Somewhere in his shallow character, he found the need to validate himself to a murderer, a soon-to-be-dead murderer— perplexing in the least; pathetic in the most.

Sandy was having the best time. A bag, literally bursting at the seams with tasty white, awaited her. In the interim, she got to watch a hated cop sweat and fidget.

Lookin' like a ho in chu'ch, Sandy thought.

"Doth protest too much methinks. We all know your little secret, and what's more, Detective Sergeant, no one cares. Your cousin keeps you on a leash. You run this way and that, bringing Ted the juicy bits. You're pitiful. And a fool."

Nate was indignant. What he lacked in smarts or courage, he made up for in hubris.

"I don't know what you're talking about," he finally managed. "Besides, you should be more worried about yourself. Ding dong, about time to get your wings clipped."

Nate smiled, satisfied. *Hah. Wings clipped. Definitely going in the report.*

"You're more of a fool than I thought."

The grunts that were Buzzkill's team signals continued over the radio as the men made their way through the structure.

"Just keep talking. Just keep on talking. Tick tock. You're a dead man."

"When God calls me, I will go. But you, Nathan Davis, will not deliver me. I warned you."

Nate scooted down in the seat, an involuntary movement borne from an aversion to large holes in his head. A horrible thought occurred to him. The junkie woman had come from the *opposite* direction of the building.

Oh no.

"Wicked."

The Angel's word was punctuated when a brilliant flash consumed the top floor of the warehouse. The blast cascaded down the building until the entire thing was burned or burning. Buzzkill's team fell completely silent.

Sandy's face was bathed in light, exposing every scar and remnant of her life on the 'row. Her smile was wide, her gaze awestruck. And just like that, Sandy (the former Emily) was gone. What remained of her head landed in Nate's lap. He screamed again.

Nate jumped from the rear bench. Bullets tore at the seats and windows of the SUV. He leaned between the front seats. Showered in glass and bits of metal, he turned the keys. He reached for the brake pedal and held it down. He threw the SUV into reverse and with both hands depressed the accelerator.

The SUV grunted in protest for half a second, then shot backward like it had been fired from a cannon. The bullets stopped tearing at the seats, but Nate kept his head low.

Once the inevitable happened and the SUV hit an embankment, Nate and the piece of Sandy's head were flung about inside. When the behemoth finally came to rest at the bottom of a spillway, Nate could hear the Angel laughing at him through the still-open flip phone. Then he heard no more.

***

From his vantage point atop a building across the street, the man had an unobstructed view of Pat's sojourn across the parking lot.

Through the Hensoldt sniper scope attached to the Heckler & Koch PSG1 sniper rifle, he could see the beads of sweat on the detective's neck as he made his way.

Unlike Pat, the man laughed aloud as various miscreants and lowlifes ran away. Despite that, his concentration remained on the detective, the crosshairs of the scope focused directly on his back. The rounds fired by the rifle would obliterate the police-issue vest, so the largest target area would suffice.

As Pat paused and looked to the sky before crossing the threshold of Widow Drake's motel room, the man readied himself for the kill shot. So immersed was he in the moment that he didn't hear another walk up behind him.

In any event, it wouldn't have mattered how well he listened as the man who moved like a panther strode up next to him. He never would have noticed him coming.

When it happened, Luis was conscious only that he was spinning; he didn't know why or how. The question remained forever unanswered when his face smashed into the concrete slab three stories below.

Widow Drake dialed the phone he'd taken from Luis's waist before tipping him over the side.

"Yeah?" Pat answered.

"If you're here in an ill-fated attempt to take me out or arrest me, tell me now."

Widow had one hand on the phone, the other on the trigger of the sniper rifle.

"Goddammit. Yep, that's it. I walked in here announcing myself to every dickhead within five blocks in some ingenious plan to kill you. Hell yeah, I'm a savant of assassination."

"At the car. And Detective, if you make me uneasy, I will kill you."

"Fuck off," Pat said, slamming down the receiver.

Widow smirked as he began his descent. When he exited, he didn't even look at the mess that used to be

Luis. Pat returned to his car much faster than he'd left it. He whistled when he saw Widow, and what Widow was standing next to.

"He was going to shoot you...or me. Probably me...after I killed you," Widow offered, holding up the sniper rifle.

Pat glanced to the rooftop and sighed.

Cloak and dagger bullshit.

"He worked for Ted Allen," Widow said.

Pat laughed. He leaned against his car and fished out a cigarette.

"Motherfucker. Of course he did," he said, still laughing.

"Funny?" Widow asked.

"Absurd," Pat answered, turning to regard his possible assassin. "So, whatcha got, Widow Drake? Why'd they point me at you?"

"I'm a wanted mass murderer," Widow stated matter-of-factly. "That, and if Ted Allen wants me dead, I can safely assume he wants Dylan Jacoby alive."

The neon sign shone with blinding clarity, and a giant piece of the puzzle fell into place. Pat's look of recognition was not missed by Widow.

"I assume you know who that is?"

Pat was about to answer when he and Widow simultaneously spied the creeper. Widow fell back under cover, forcing his way into the adjacent office building, before Pat had noticed he'd moved. Pat followed suit just as the blacked-out SUV roared toward them.

They got inside an instant before bullets sprayed the area.

"Fucking cloak and dagger bullshit," Pat yelled over the sound of machine-gun fire.

[END OF PART III]

PART IV:
28

Rosie sat alone at the massive dining table. After he'd *rescued* her from police headquarters, Ted spent most of the drive interrogating her, followed by several minutes of thoughtful silence before he began a new battery of questions. When they'd arrived at his estate, Ted had deposited her in the dining room. He'd offered no option for sleeping, despite the late hour, and Rosie had requested none before Ted disappeared.

Now, mentally and physically exhausted, she thumbed at an expensive tray of cheeses, absentmindedly swirling wine in the Bordeaux glass until she spilled deep red directly onto the brilliant white tablecloth.

"Shit."

Out of nowhere, two tuxedo-clad, thin, bald men appeared. One of them mumbled something, almost certainly an insult, in a language Rosie didn't understand and cleaned the spill so completely no trace of stain remained. The other replaced the tray and put a less-full glass of wine in place of the one she'd spilled.

"Must be nice," she said.

"Yes, it is."

Rosie looked up from the spread, down the length of the table. Draped in a silk robe and nightgown, which even from a great distance looked so refined Rosie was sure they had a room full of silkworms tucked somewhere in the mansion, was Laura Allen, Ted's illustrious wife.

"But it isn't free," Laura added.

Rosie got the distinct impression she wasn't talking about monetary cost.

Laura glided to a seat next to Rosie, and one of the same tuxedo-clad men appeared to pull it out for her. The second brought a tray of assorted chocolates and two flutes of white wine.

"Ted really has no clue what makes a woman tick," she said, offering Rosie the sweets.

Suddenly ravenous, Rosie stuffed the delectable treats in her mouth. She could imagine her grandmother saying, "Gurl, you know you wasn't raised in a barn. Eat like a lady."

Rosie laughed aloud at the thought. Bits of nut, chocolate, and fruit covered the tablecloth. No sooner had her chuckles started than they morphed into sobs, powerful, body-wracking sobs. She wanted to stop them, wanted desperately to regain her composure in Ted Allen's house, in front of his wife. But the train had already gone off the cliff. There was no reining in this particular emotional tide.

She didn't feel like a person anymore. She had become a tool. Used by the police, the Angel, and Ted. To be borrowed or stolen, and discarded when her purpose was served.

Laura regarded the poor woman at her dining table, covered in snot, drool, and half-eaten bits of expensive chocolate, and cradled her head to her chest. She rubbed her back and rocked slowly back and forth, all the while humming.

As Rosie calmed slightly, she began to recognize that, at present, she was drooling and crying into the bosom of Laura Allen. She attempted to recoil. As if expecting that, Laura tightened her grip. Rosie relented and fell fully into her. She wrapped her hands around Laura's waist and together they waited for the train to find the bottom of the chasm.

"My husband can have that effect," Laura said after a few minutes.

Rosie sat up and wiped her eyes. She was only slightly startled when the tuxedo-clad twins appeared next to her, one holding a warm, wet washcloth, the other a tray of loose chamomile leaves, a hot kettle, and two cups and saucers.

Rosie cleaned herself. She made a cup of tea and offered one to Laura, to which Laura displayed her glass of wine. Rosie closed her eyes and held the teacup to her nose. She breathed in the flowery aroma and took a few measured sips. There was no rush in her manner and no request for speed forthcoming from her companion.

Laura had seen this scene play out many times—though not in the privacy of her home, or at this level of undress, *or* with any concern. Some days you see the homeless man and say to yourself, "That's why you don't do crack." Other times you buy him a meal. Laura had long ago stopped trying to figure out her feelings, instead learning to trust them.

"He can. He definitely can. But I did this to myself," Rosie said.

Indeed, you did, Laura thought without judgment.

Hee hee, Rosie's departed grandmother added.

Rosie hung her head and sighed hard. She ran her hands through her hair and sighed again.

"My dear," Laura started, "accepting responsibility for your circumstance is only the beginning."

Rosie sat up and placed her hands in her lap. Her countenance was one of a student.

"You must own it. Look, Rosie, I will spend the rest of my life with a man who can never want me as I want him. That's not a sacrifice; it's a choice. My choice. Right now, you're asking yourself 'how could you', 'why did you'. There are no hows or whys, there is only now...and what you do next. So tell me, what do you do?" the wife of Rosie's benefactor asked.

The next step is yo' firs' step, Grandmama added.

"I don't know. I suppose I try to get out of this mess with more self-respect than I came into it with," Rosie answered.

Laura smiled. Rosie looked into her face, for the

first time really, and responded to her smile with total bewilderment.

Rosie had, during her investigation into Ted Allen, seen his better half perhaps half a dozen times in person, and dozens more in pictures. Other than a few ancillary facts, she realized she didn't know much about Laura Allen. She knew Laura came from old money; her father's family owned a national auto parts chain, and her mother's family had made a fortune in oil. Either she'd been so focused on Ted that she hadn't bothered to pay attention to the trophy on his arm, or—and perhaps more accurately—Laura Allen wore a public mask. Literally, because the woman applied a *lot* of makeup, though not a trace of it was currently evident, and figuratively, because none of the qualities of character, so obvious here, had ever been hinted at before. Rosie, like most, had assumed she was a strikingly beautiful, dimwitted heiress, who read sparingly and spoke less.

Laura noticed the look and laughed. A classy, deep, under-control laugh, not the hen hackle Rosie would have previously assumed she would utter.

"We all play a role, my dear," she said, patting Rosie's hand. "The only question is, do you define the role or let it define you?"

Laura stood and turned, leaving a dumbfounded *and* impressed Rosie to regard her departure.

"When you are ready, they will show you to your room," Laura said without turning. "I expect we will speak tomorrow. I'm sure my husband will want to as well. Be sure you've had a good night's sleep."

Rosie was supposed to say "thank you" or "I will" or any number of pleasantries appropriate given Laura's recent kindness. Instead she asked a question, equally naked in compassion and incredulity.

"*You* married Ted Allen?"

Laura paused at the threshold, her hand already on the butler's door.

"You know, Eva truly loved Adolf."

The door swung closed with Rosie still staring at the space where Laura had stood. For a minute longer, she sat rigid before shaking herself free from hypnosis. She rose and was immediately joined by the tuxedo twins. She followed them mindlessly through winding corridors until they stopped outside of a door. She walked several feet beyond them before realizing she was alone. The twins waited with barely concealed irritation. When she returned, they opened the French doors, waited for Rosie to enter, and closed them behind her without a word.

Rosie hurried across the apartment-sized guest room and fell onto the bed. She meant to get the sleep Laura had suggested. She kicked off her shoes and curled up in the sheets.

Yeah, an' both of them got blowed up. How'd dat work out?

Rosie grinned, the return of her grandmother's voice making her feel more secure that she had at the very least started to walk the right path, and closed her eyes.

29

Pat McConnell had served in the military. He wasn't old enough to have been in Vietnam, but did see combat in a few peacekeeping missions. He'd been shot at under the flag *and* the badge. In either instance, it sucked.

This sucked worse.

The men outside advanced on the building in a firing line. There was no pause in the barrage. Streams of light now shone through giant holes in the cinder block exterior like spotlights. The interior walls were obliterated, throwing a blinding dust cloud into the air. Pieces of the ceiling rained down on them like a biblical torrent. The noise was deafening.

Pat glanced at his newest partner. Widow lay on his back with his head propped up against the side of a desk. The man looked like he was lounging under a palm tree on the beach. Pat yelled something at his too-cool-for-school companion. Neither of them heard him over the racket, though Pat doubted Widow would've responded even if he could. He ignored him for the moment and searched for a way out of the death trap.

I can't see shit.

When the men outside finally ceased their fire, Pat went to poke his head up. In that instant, Widow pushed him back down and jumped to his feet. Even with a gunshot wound, the man moved with astounding grace. Silently, he rushed toward the rear of the building. With a pistol in each hand, he shot the wall on each side of the doorway three times—two shots on a line about six inches apart and a third above them, forming a triangle. The men waiting in ambush came down like felled trees, stiff and tall. They were both dead before they hit the ground.

Annoyed, particularly at being pushed, Pat was about to move in kind when Widow yelled for him to stay down. The order proved unnecessary. The second Widow disappeared through the doorway, the firing squad began anew.

"Fuck you, Carl Phillips," Pat screamed.

There were several others worthy of scorn—Ted Allen just for being him and Widow Drake for leaving him to die—but really, he wanted to hear himself curse his father's old friend, the man who'd looked him in the eye and sent him to his death.

"Goddammit."

Pat got into a crouch and readied himself. He would not die cowering. *At least one of you is coming with.*

Against every intelligent fiber of his being, Pat forced himself in the direction of the gunfire. Even when one of the shells scorched a line of blood and burned skin down his left arm, he kept going. When he reached the entrance, he took a deep breath, cursed *them all,* and went.

He unloaded four rounds into the closest man, who pointed his assault rifle at an upward trajectory. Every shot found the mark, and the man crumpled to the ground. Pat scanned the street and saw that among the scores of glittering shell casings, four other bodies lay still.

Half a minute later, Widow emerged from the building, carrying an assault rifle that matched the mercs'.

"They're finished. Let's go."

Widow fled down the street. While Pat stood outside, alone among the five dead mercenaries and the two others inside the building, two things became abundantly clear: One, the man who had obviously adopted the stupid moniker *Widow* should have added an "er" to it, and two, Ted *and* Carl had meant for him to die tonight. The latter thought chased him all the way to Widow's waiting car.

"Ted Allen," Widow said when Pat climbed in the passenger seat.

Widow drove without headlights through various alleys and side streets, avoiding both oncoming police cruisers and the eyes in the sky. On another day, Pat would've been impressed with the psychopath's unending skill set, but at that moment he was so angry he couldn't see straight. He went to retrieve a cigarette from his pocket and noticed he was still holding the Glock.

He thought back to earlier in the day, before he knew he was ensnared in the world of espionage and assassins—back when he was just a normal cop chasing down leads and killers. He remembered what his fat, always positive partner and friend had reminded him. He holstered the weapon and grabbed what he needed to *get his head back in the game.*

"Dylan Jacoby," he corrected through a cloud of smoke.

Widow shrugged as if the delay meant nothing to him.

"Okay. Then Ted Allen," he said.

30

The man wasn't resting. Not really. Though he'd been casket-still for hours, save a slight tremor across his exposed chest when he inhaled, his eyes never closed.

Nor, however, did he see.

His vision was clouded, obscured by faces contorted in fear, in agony, and finally, in death. He believed the soul departed when the vessel expired, but he *knew* part of the spirit lingered. Whenever Dylan saw a dead animal—a deer in the bed of a pickup, a squirrel sent to oblivion on the roadside, a rabbit crushed in the jaws of his dog, or that same dog when she'd died in his lap—they always had the same look on their face: dark eyes, mouth slightly open, a discolored, mildly bloated tongue hanging. There was never any indication of how the animal had died left on its face.

In the world of the sentient, however, things worked differently. If death had come with contentment, acceptance, and peace, anyone who gazed upon the lifeless body instantly knew it. When, however, it came under less-agreeable circumstances, the same was true. More so. The men and women he killed, wretches though they may have been, always left a piece of their soul around, with him. Forever.

Initially, Dylan tried to ignore their lifeless gazes, to concentrate only on his mission, a divine mission, because he would not be distracted by the living *or* the dead. And initially, he succeeded. But as the numbers climbed, the toll of the dead on the living rose in kind. His resolve began to falter. Now, on the cusp of the day of retribution, he gave himself over fully to the memories.

The cup hath run over.

The beginning, an ordeal: He let the random screams he could no longer ignore take shape. The choked gasps from Juicy's cracked and blood-smeared lips, the whimper of Hollis, the bubbled wails of Mariam that he could hear even as her weighted body sunk deeper into the lake, the horrified cries of disbelief muffled by dirt-packed mouths, and all the others he'd dispatched assailed him in unison.

A single note of rage, and yet each individually discernable. A composition of misery ostensibly authored by righteousness, a deafening cacophony.

He covered his ears. The wailing refused to desist. He screamed. The vengeful chorus simply reached a heightened note, an unyielding crescendo of earsplitting sadism. He writhed as his stomach wrenched in a thousand knots of moral consequence. By the time he fell from the bed, his chest and face covered in vomit-stained spittle, his pained screams were nothing more than pitiful groans.

The muscled, imposing man, this proud Gideon, the bringer of death, destroyer of the wicked, now cradled his knees to his chest and wept.

The middle, the nadir: Through a pitch-black flood of regret and doubt, Dylan saw a way to silence the demons of his past. In a room bereft of light, black against black, the instrument of Dylan's relief called to him. The discordant racket inexplicably blended into a soothing harmony of encouragement.

If by staining my hands with the blood of evil men, I consign my soul to share their fate...so be it.

His body wracked by self-inflicted strain, Dylan pushed himself onto all fours. Though the pistol was only a few yards away, it seemed no amount of crawling brought him any closer to it. He wondered morbidly if he'd already done it and was *already* in Hell. Was he to spend an eternity tortured by a sliver of hope inside a hopeless predicament?

When his fingers found purchase upon deliverance, he didn't exalt. The big man collapsed. His tears were spent, his energy expended, his hope renewed. There was no correction of position, no hesitation in action. Dylan pulled the trigger the moment his face hit the floor.

The end, taken as providence: Dylan had meant to meet his end wide-eyed, but in the instant, he couldn't resist the very human response to shut his lids, to flinch against the inevitable. In his last moment on the Earth, he cowered, and the bullet did not quite reach its mark.

Nevertheless, Dylan Jacoby was dead. Dark blood pooled below his head, crimson highlights against his now sweat-spiked blond hair. Blazing shrapnel embedded in his cheek and forehead, burning and charring in virtually the same instant, bestowing the man with dark scars to match the eyes that had seen fit to judge life and death, hardening the jawline of a man burdened with God's purpose.

What had once been Dylan Jacoby was dead.

When the Angel opened his eyes, he felt no pain from his injury nor shame at the reason for it. He turned over and stared at the ceiling, peaceful. The chorus began anew. Each voice clamoring to be louder, more incisive than the others. He smiled, sort of, as best he could. He waved his hand. At once, the voices ceased.

Go now, to whatever eternity God deems.

He stayed on the ground, lying in a pool of his own blood until the first evidence of the beginnings of dawn peeked through the sides of the heavy curtains.

"A night of revelation. A day of retribution," he said.

He got up and walked to the shower. In scalding water, he burned off the remnants of the trial: the vomit, the blood, the tears, the smell of doubt and fear. He stepped from the shower and wiped the mirror, seeing himself for the first time. He caressed the raised welt along his forehead and cheek with slow, deliberate strokes—almost lovingly. Using his tongue, he traced the path of the bullet through his other cheek, most of which was lying on the floor inside the bedroom. Several teeth were completely gone, and part of his jaw was lodged inside his gums. He could frown and speak, but he couldn't smile, not in any way a human being would consider joyous. The smile now resembled the snarl of a fang-bearing animal. The shrapnel gave him stripes to match. *Tasmanian Devil*, he thought.

A devil.

Fitting. Since I am already found guilty, why should I struggle in vain?

He got dressed and walked downstairs to the kitchen.

"Dylan."

He ignored the voice. He went over to the automatic coffee pot. The voice persisted as he poured. He put the mug to his lips and drank. The hot liquid found every wound inside his mouth. The pain was exquisite. The Angel didn't recoil. His eyes closed, only to absorb the pain, not to succumb to it. When he placed the empty mug on the counter, he turned to regard the voice.

"Dylan, please."

"You don't deserve this?"

"Of course not. Dylan, are you insane?"

In that moment, the Angel looked up into the blushed and bloated face of the man balancing on a tabletop, his neck cinched in a noose.

When Deputy Mayor Chris Watson looked down into his friend's mangled face and eyes, he saw a complete lack of humanity. The terror of a night spent balancing precariously on a tabletop with his neck tied, listening to ominous, almost supernatural-sounding screams and groans coming from his guest room, felt inconsequential.

Now he knew terror.

"Dylan, please."

The Angel walked over to Chris. He stood just below him and stared at him, through him.

"You have sinned. You have taken with malice and disregard that which God has deemed precious."

Chris shook his head. Not so much in denial, but in shock and amazement. He was so incredulous he nearly lost his footing and fell from the table.

"Dylan, you bastard. That was an accident. You know goddamn well it was an accident. *You*! You prick, *you* decided it wasn't my fault. That kid ran out in front of me."

"You were drunk."

"So were you. Goddamn you, Dylan. You asshole. It was an accident. You said so. Kill yourself, you hypocrite. *Dylan!*"

The Angel said a prayer, drowned out by Chris screaming at him, then screaming for help, and finally, just screaming.

"Dylan—"

"Is dead," the Angel finished.

He kicked the table away. He turned his back on

Chris Watson while the man struggled with the thick rope. He went about the business of calmly collecting the things he'd brought to his friends' home after a night of adventures, while that same friend bucked and kicked, lips blue, eyes bloodshot. The Angel left the house through the kitchen without another glance back.

"A great day. A Godly day it will be," he said.

31

Father Walter Brown sat at the bay window inside the bartender's apartment. The morning sun cresting over the horizon splayed golden streaks on the surface of the Mississippi River. The sweet lady had spent the night serving him copious amounts of whiskey. He'd only recently found out her name was Rebecca, and she was at the moment in the bathroom washing a night's worth of smoke, drink, and the occasional man's hands off her.

Lost in his own world, Walter jumped when Rebecca appeared behind him with two glasses. She wore an oversized Cardinals jersey, unbuttoned far enough for a glimpse if one was so inclined, and bright green wool socks. Her hair was still damp. Drops of water fell from its tips, traveling down the side of her face, around her round eyes, over the hump of her cheekbones to the corners of her mouth, illuminating her full, pink lips before pausing inside the dimple on her chin, and then, at last, falling to her chest. Walter's head literally snapped down, following the path of a mesmerizing droplet. Rebecca watched the spectacle with thinly veiled amusement.

The priest was suddenly very interested in the drinks she held. She handed him the red one and sat cross-legged on the coffee table. Walter grabbed it, shut his eyes, and gulped madly. When he took the glass, he'd assumed it to be a Bloody Mary. It did have tomato juice. It was *not* a Bloody Mary.

He gagged and coughed uncontrollably. He jumped from the chair, fanning his mouth, and pushed the drink away.

"Thank you," he said.

"Hah. That's my secret recipe to kill a hangover and clear your head. Now drink it down."

Walter looked into the glass and noticed it was actually smoking. He grimaced and put it to his mouth. Rebecca tipped it up, forcing him to drink more.

"Burns, don't it?" she teased while sipping what Walter was sure was a cool, refreshing screwdriver.

He tried to reply, but his singed tongue refused to cooperate. Rebecca giggled. With his eyes and nose running, mouth salivating like a rabid dog, Walter found his seat again. He put his head between his legs and gagged a few more times into a napkin. Eventually, the fire in his mouth moved to his belly, which somehow made it more palatable. His coughing fit finally subsiding, he wiped his face as best he could with the soiled towelette and stared at his hostess.

"Why on Earth would you do that to me?"

Rebecca's unwavering smile in the midst of his

torture further infuriated the priest.

"Worked, didn't it?"

He almost admitted the accuracy of her observation, but then licked his lips, reigniting the inferno, and demurred.

"So what's the word, Wally?" she asked.

"What do you mean?"

Rebecca reclined on her hands and threw her head back, emitting a loud, obnoxious laugh. The movement only served to pull her jersey open even more.

Perhaps clarity isn't the best thing, Walter thought.

"What do you mean?" he asked again, keeping his eyes averted.

Rebecca stopped laughing, leaned forward, and— thankfully for the vacillating priest—pulled her shirt together.

"Look, Wally, I been doing this a long time. Only one o' two reasons a man comes to my bar looking like you looked yesterday. Either you know something or you did something."

Walter's wide-eyed expression was all the validation she needed.

"Now I'm not thinking you're the type to do something. I mean, you got it in you, like all o' us, but I'm not thinking you done did anything too, too bad. So I'd say you know something that did happen or 'bout to happen."

Walter was aghast. He was unaccustomed to being

on this side of the conversation. As long as he could remember, his revelations had come from study, meditation, communion with his God, or even friends of the cloth—never a vessel that looked or sounded remotely like Rebecca.

"And I figure if you know something, it's 'cause somebody done blabbed it to you. I know ya'll got that attorney-client privilege thing in your line o' work, so that puts you in a bind now, don't it? You picked the wrong job. Guy tells me he stepping out on his ol' lady, I can tell her. I don't, but I could," she said with a smile.

Walter stared out the window again. A reflection of the brilliant yellow sphere shimmered across the surface of the muddy water. He inexplicably went to take another drink from the glass when Rebecca placed her hand on his wrist, saving him from another agonizing round. Even while seated, his knees weakened at her touch.

"What's the word, Wally?" she repeated.

His mouth opened and shut without a sound. He shook his head and grunted.

"I don't know what to do. People are going to die."

"People always die," she countered. "Question you should be askin' yourself, how you want to live?"

With that, Rebecca lifted Walter's chin. They stared into each other's eyes. When she grinned at him, Walter knew firsthand the weakness that had gripped David at the sight of Bathsheba. *His* temptress leaned forward and put her lips on his forehead, right between his eyes. When she kissed him, the priest exhaled, raspy and wanting.

Rebecca left him, eyes closed, alone at the window.

"Wally, you can sit there feeling sorry for yourself all day if you want. Drink yourself silly. Lord knows I've done it before. Or you can figure a way outta the mess you're in that you can live with."

"I love you," he said.

Even without turning, he could tell she was smiling. He could feel it.

"Wally, honey," she said.

He turned to regard her. She was posed seductively in the doorway to her bedroom.

"There's always the other option," she said.

She stayed there for just an instant, long enough for any remaining color to drain from his cheeks. A frisky smile on her face, she gave him a wink before she backed into the room.

She closed the door behind her.

Thank God.

He placed the devil drink on the table and walked to the door. He held the knob a long time before he pulled it open and stepped out of her apartment.

He recited the Lord's Prayer aloud as he walked down the stairs and onto the street. By the end of the passage, he noticed he was running. Fast and with conviction. There wasn't much time.

"Let me tell you, Father Brown, how retribution falls upon the wicked," Dylan Jacoby had told him.

Father Brown broke into a full-out sprint.

32

"No good," Pat said.

A shrug was Widow's only response. Pat glared at the man seated at his kitchen table. He was annoyed about Widow Drake, irritated that he owed the man— psychopathic assassin that he was—his life. Two times over. It made him mad that Widow was sitting in Lou's seat and the fat detective with the overgrown mustache wasn't. He was angry that things had gotten so messed up that he *needed* Widow to finish this.

But at present, he was mostly mad that *the cocksucker isn't even listening to me.*

"Hey, I'm talking to you here."

A slight nostril flare was the only indication Widow had heard.

You're pissed. Good, cause I'm fucking livid.

"It's FUBAR," Pat continued. "You, my crazy little friend, have been publicly named the Angel. Or at least you will be when the winner of the leak race gets to a phone. And me, well, fucking-A, I'm whatcha call persona non grata. Former lead detective on the

Angel case spotted with Angel suspect. Just great."

Widow was unmoved by Pat's news. He simply stared at the worn-down detective as if waiting for him to say something of significance.

"Well? You got anything to say?" Pat demanded.

"Depends."

"On what, motherfucker?" Pat seethed as he straddled a chair across from Widow.

"On whether you're finished whining."

Pat's entire body tensed. He squeezed the back of the chair so hard the old wood audibly cracked. He glared while Widow looked on impassively. At least his face was impassive. His eyes were a different story.

Pat smirked and relaxed. He unpeeled his fingers from the chair and leaned back. Through a haze of smoke, he gestured for Widow to go ahead.

The assassin shrugged. "You've told me nothing. If you don't want to reveal the Angel, I'm the obvious choice. I should've figured it out. If I was in my right mind I would've gone to see Ted, blacked out both his eyes, and left town, never to be heard from again. But I wasn't in my right mind, and because of that I allowed Ted Allen to make two pathetic attempts on my life. Three, including you."

"Thanks, asshole."

"What I don't understand is why not?" Widow continued.

"Why not what, smart guy?"

"Who's Dylan Jacoby to Ted? Mayors smoke crack,

presidents get blown by interns. So Jacoby's a former prosecutor... Why's Ted give a shit about him being the Angel?"

It was Pat's turn to flash a superior look. "Ted doesn't give a shit, tough guy. But I bet Dylan's father does." He looked down into his lap and sighed.

"Really? You're going to milk this?"

But Pat wasn't milking the moment. He was far away, back in the old neighborhood. Sixteen years old, already very much the recalcitrant asshole he would remain some thirty years later. Like any self-respecting rebellious son of a decorated police detective, Pat sat with the other wayward youths on the edge of the playground, smoking cigarettes and drinking beer. A group of the so-called *good kids* was playing a game of stick ball.

As games filled with pubescent males are wont to do, the competition got out of hand, and a much bigger kid found the smallest kid to vent his frustrations on.

Pat, mild lawbreaker, was still the son of a cop, and he hated bullies. He was making his way across the field before the first punch was thrown. But by the time Pat made it to the melee, the bully was on the ground with a bleeding lip, swollen eyes, and a nose that—even to the uninitiated—looked broken.

The little kid didn't say a word to his fallen foe. He simply turned to the others and asked if they wanted to play again. That kid didn't stay small forever. As a man, he was as physically imposing as his father, and like the young Pat, he always hated bullies. He'd joined the army to protect the world from bullies. And when he came home to St. Louis, law degree in hand, he became an assistant district attorney.

"Jacoby is his mother's last name," Pat finally said, returning to the present. "His father was quite fond of new tail. Divorced years ago. And he wasn't just a prosecutor. He was a goddamn force of nature. He went from violent and sex offenders to white collar crimes—going after big fish. And no matter where he was, he had the grand jury handing out indictments like candy. He got convictions; he kicked ass."

Widow's interest in the trip down memory lane was fast waning, but he remained curious about the end. "So, what happened to the wonder boy?" he asked.

"Ted Allen."

Widow's eyebrows arched. *Well, now, this is interesting.*

"Dylan had Ted dead to rights on enough shit to back up the Mississippi: fraud, embezzlement, bribery. If it was here and shady, he tied Ted to it. Dylan was good, but..."

"Ted is better," Widow finished.

"Yeah," Pat sighed. *Weak knees, empty bank accounts, and a guy who thought he could fly.*

"Everybody's got skeletons, and Ted found 'em all. Everything was falling apart, but Dylan still had one ace: a guy who wouldn't turn. Used to be a fed. He wasn't even on the case—hell, he wasn't even local— for him the shit was personal. Once he got to work, files came up missing from Ted's offices. Confidential stories and pictures of Ted made it into the paper. Whenever another witness was suddenly forgetful or some paperwork was accidentally shredded, the guy found something else. Dylan had to know the shit was dirty, but fuck it, he was taking down Ted Allen. Anyway, eventually it all went sideways. Dylan's informant jumped from the balcony of his hotel room, and Dylan got his ass kicked in court. Lotta heads rolled."

"Dylan?"

"Hah, not exactly," Pat said. "Dylan, he got promoted to DA. He was already earmarked for it and, hell, it *was* only one ass kicking. But the magic was gone. The office went to shit. Losses, pleading shit out. He oversaw the clown show for a few years, then he walked."

Widow watched Pat more than he listened. And what he saw troubled him. Admiration. Disappointment. Regret.

"The guy helping him committed suicide? You believe that?"

"No one else ever went into his room. Door dead-bolted from the inside. Yeah, it had to be unless Houdini did the deed."

"Maybe," Widow said doubtfully.

Pat was looking down when Widow spoke. He stared at a cigarette cherry dancing around inside his fingers, which suddenly wouldn't stop vibrating.

The hands always knew first. Widow had just

given himself away.

"Or someone just as good at their job as Ted is at his tossed the fat man off the twenty-story balcony and left without a trace," Pat offered smoothly. The quiver ceased.

"Dylan's man was ex-CIA, by the way," Widow countered.

Pat looked up. Slowly.

The assassin's eyes were always fierce, but the rest of him was carefully arranged to convey utter, almost bored, relaxation. The detective now saw past this.

The tips of Widow's fingers were colorless where he'd laid them flat against the table, coiled and ready to pounce. The blood pushed back under his nails. *Your move, Detective.*

The men stared at each other across the small, nondescript kitchen table. They were close enough to hold hands. In *reality*, they stood on opposite sides of the chasm of morality where justice and punishment waged war in perpetuity.

"Anyway, he was born Dylan Phillips—and Mayor Carl Phillips is his father," Pat said finally.

The color returned to Widow's fingertips.

"Well," Widow said as he stood, "let's go."

"Where?"

"To where we'll find Mr. Jacoby."

They left Pat's apartment and awaited the elevator in silence.

"After this is over, you and me, we're gonna dance," Pat said without regarding Widow.

A toothy grin was Widow's only response.
The cat baring his teeth.

33

Rosie awoke with a start. The fine sheets, oversized bed, and spacious surroundings all felt foreign to her. It took her several seconds to remember where she was.

As unease abated, a sense of purpose took its place. She pushed the sheets off and sat on the edge of the bed. On the adjacent table was a tray of assorted pastries and every option of breakfast beverage imaginable. Draped across a chair was a set of clothes, business attire. She didn't even have to check; she knew they'd be her size.

"Think of everything don't you, Ted?" she said.

As she spoke, the French doors opened, and one of the twins entered.

"Master Allen will see you in twenty minutes."

The twin left without reply.

"Hmph." Rosie rolled her eyes and stuffed a croissant in her mouth.

Despite the luxuriousness of the shower, she finished in record time and was escorted by the other twin to Ted's quarters in fifteen minutes—not because Ted wanted her there, but because it was *her* call. She could hear the voices long before they reached the door.

"You sonuvabitch, you tried to kill my boy."

"Carl, get ahold of yourself. I did no such thing," Ted replied.

"You sent a strike team at my son!"

Rosie's escort knocked, interrupting whatever retort Ted would've given.

"Come."

Rosie was ushered into the room where Ted Allen and Mayor Carl Phillips sat on opposing couches. At least she thought it was Mayor Carl Phillips. In her capacity as a political beat reporter, she'd seen Carl Phillips up close and personal multiple times. He was always the large man with an outsized personality to match, able to charm or coerce his most ardent detractors. The man in front of her, shrinking inside his suit with reddened eyes and a ring of antacid around his mouth, bore little resemblance to the mayor she'd come to know.

Ted Allen looked like he always looked, as though he was a model taken from a Giorgio Armani catalogue.

Rosie wasn't a detective, and right now didn't think she was even that good of a reporter, but even a child knows two plus two is four.

"Your son...he's the Angel. My God," she said before thinking.

"Rosie, I trust you slept well," Ted said.

"Who the hell are you?" the mayor said.

"I did. Thank you," she answered. "Mr. Mayor, my name is—"

"Fine, fine," Ted broke in. "This is Rosalind Williams. She's in my employ and a player in our little game here."

"Oh yeah, the *reporter.*"

Ted beckoned Rosie to a seat. He then recounted his version of events since she'd last been apprised, including and up to the failed attempt on Widow and Pat. For purposes of the ruse, he continued to refer to the incident at the warehouse as a failed capture, as opposed to a failed kill.

As Ted regaled her with his tale, the stark differences in demeanor between the two men became even more obvious. More than simply being dapper, Ted had an excited twinkle in his eyes. It'd been there since he'd first spoken to her in the car, but now his eyes were positively sparkling.

My God, how long ago that seems, she thought.

"So, it's been quite the night. Sentiments?"

Rosie didn't answer immediately. Not for lack of words. She had plenty. But the fact that Ted Allen was asking anybody for input threw her.

When you eva seen a show off do it fo' nobody?

Rosie smiled. Ted smiled wider. Carl looked at both like they were crazy, then at Ted like he was evil.

"Everything?"

Ted heard the implication. It delighted him.

"Why not?"

"Well, Ted," she said, leaning forward in her chair, "I'd say it depends on what game you're playing and how badly you want to win."

Ted stiffened slightly. His gaze bored into Rosie. She didn't flinch. She cocked her head, raised her eyebrows, and calmly waited for him to respond. The mayor downed another bottle of antacid.

Das righ', baby. In fo' a penny, in fo' a pound.

"The only one worth playing," Ted said after a moment. "And...I don't play to lose."

"What the hell are you two talking about? This is no game. This is my boy. My boy."

Ted and Rosie barely acknowledged the mayor. Rosie knew enough of Ted Allen to understand what had happened. Surely the mayor was tormented by his son—what he had done, what he'd become. But there was something else. She'd been seduced into Ted Allen's game herself, so she knew Carl Phillips was here because Ted owned him, not the other way around. He was defined by his role.

Ain't neva a honest man in a con game. Always lookin' fo' sometin fo' free.

"Do you have other men?" Rosie inquired.

"There are always more men," Ted answered, his smile growing wider, if that was possible.

"Then you have two options. You can have your men give last night another go. Or..." Rosie paused.

The effect on Ted was exhilarating. He was having the time of his life. No, this was not chess.

"Or you could just wait for him here."

The mayor showed more life than he had in a long time. His head snapped up, and his eyes danced furiously back and forth between them. The color drained from his face, only to return as realization dawned. He wagged his finger at Ted. Spittle pooled at the corners of his mouth. He tried to form the words but anger forced them back down.

Watching Carl be riled and broken by emotions and the sense of coulda, woulda, shoulda almost drove Ted to laugh aloud, long and hard with youthful abandon. Instead, he gazed at Carl with a look of concern, which barely masked the contempt he felt for his one-time adversary.

"You. You know where he's going?"

"I do," Ted answered, his voice quiet.

"Then why, why? Why the hell didn't you just wait for him there? What the hell was all that last night?"

"A necessary risk," Ted said.

"Damn you, Ted Allen. I'm—"

"Why didn't *you*?" Rosie asked, suddenly angry.

Carl whirled to face the woman he'd forgotten was there. He glared in her direction, his eyes barely more than slits.

"Why didn't I what?" Carl paused after every word, the promise of imminent punishment made evident.

Rosie was unbothered. She'd been in short order hired, threatened, beaten, almost raped, illegally detained, and nearly broken, *but* she'd come out the other side. The man in front of her, literally towering over her, was of little consequence and even less significance.

"Mr. Mayor, you could have, at the very moment you were given this information, gone directly to the police. How about your handpicked chief? Instead, of the myriad of options available to you, you chose Ted Allen. You were willing to let a detective be killed and God knows how many other people. You turned your back on every duty you're sworn to uphold."

Rosie shook her head. "I get it. He's your son. Having said that, Mr. Mayor, I think your opportunity to ask why expired twenty-four hours ago."

Ted beamed. He was as proud in that moment as he'd ever been of another human being. *My, my, look at what I've created.*

Carl fell back into the couch, resigned to ride the wave he'd helped start, hoping beyond reason that his son would come away intact.

"Rosie," Ted said with actual affection, "will you excuse us, please?"

Rosie stood, saluted both men, and stepped into the hallway. Laura was waiting.

"Perhaps our talk won't be needed after all," Laura said.

"Oh, I don't know about that," Rosie replied. "Postponed."

"Postponed then," Laura said as she turned.

She was almost out of sight when Rosie called to her.

"I need to make a call. A private call," she said.

Laura leaned back against the wall. She crossed her arms and beamed.

Look at what I've found, she thought.

She snapped her fingers, and a twin appeared. He took the instructions and led Rosie to Laura's office. Rosie went to the desk and dialed.

"Yeah, what?"

34

"How'd you figure this anyhow?" Pat asked Widow as he drove.

"You people are so simple. Frankly, you're just as elementary as the idiots you spend your lives chasing."

Pat let the insult pass.

"Once I surmised his identity."

"You mean once he shot your ass up," Pat retorted.

Widow sighed. "Be that as it may, after that it was easy. Every victim, save the two would-be robbers on Whispering Hollow, was from a case his office tried and lost, or pleaded out. Apparently, your Mr. Jacoby equates a tie with a loss."

"I can understand that," Pat agreed.

"I'm sure you can."

"Whoa there, cowboy. Don't go putting me in the same boat as this jackass. Dylan Jacoby ain't some righteous hand of justice or some shit. He's a sore loser with daddy issues and a God complex. Him and me got nothing in common, you got that?"

"Anyway" Widow continued as if Pat had said

nothing, "he's obviously just working his way back through lost cases. And that brings us to Mr. Maxwell. Up on the right."

Widow slowed the car to a crawl. The block was filled with matching one-story, cottage-style homes, each built on a hill. In the early morning hours, the area was stone quiet.

They exited the car a few houses up from the Maxwell residence.

"You know him. Do not hesitate. He will kill you."

"Your concern is touching," Pat replied.

"Two is better than one," Widow said. "Give me ninety seconds. We breach together."

Pat was about to say something about this being his operation, but Widow was already up the hill and through the gangway between houses before he could get the words out. Despite the narrow passage being full of clutter, Widow made only slightly more noise than an alley cat would have.

Pat was almost to the house when a car turned onto the street. He ducked behind a minivan and fingered the trigger of the Glock as the vehicle crept closer. A few moments later, it came to a stop across the street.

Ninety seconds was long gone. Pat knew Widow was already in the house, alone. The play was made.

He's a big boy.

The occupant got out. Pat glanced through the window discreetly.

Dylan? Right size. Can't be sure. Dammit.

Pat's breathing slowed. His senses peaked. His muscles coiled. He crouched down farther, pointing the Glock in the direction he knew the man would come. He came into view: black clothes, blond hair kept short. Tall and muscular.

Dylan, Pat thought.

A sense of relief started to creep. He buried it under a grimace and exploded from his crouch, pulling the hammer back and shouting orders. He slammed into the man just as he was turning.

With his goddamn hands raised.

They crashed to the ground. Pat landed on top of him. He had one knee on his back and the Glock to the back of his head.

"Please, please. Don't do it, man. I got it. I got the money. I did just what he said, and I got the money. I even killed the kid. Dumped the bodies behind the Cheetah inside the dumpster. Come on, man, I can take you right there. Don't do it, man. Come on," the man said.

He spoke so fast it took Pat a second to register what he'd actually said.

"I'm police, you fucking idiot," Pat said.

The man's eyes widened once he quieted long enough to comprehend with whom he was speaking.

"I...," he started.

"Shut the fuck up. Name," Pat hissed.

"You police. For real? Shit. Nah, man."

"Name," Pat repeated.

He punctuated the request by pressing the Glock

harder into the man's head.

"Ahhh, man. Neal Maxwell. And I ain't saying shit else without a lawyer."

Pat leaned down on him, eliciting a grunt, and retrieved the semi-automatic .45 tucked inside his belt. Pat got off the man, keeping both pistols trained on his back.

"Get up."

"You wasting your time. No warrant. Police brutality. My lawyer is gonna have your badge. Shit ain't over."

Neal spoke again in his rapid-fire manner, but this time, Pat had no problem catching the words. He was still on a roll when his own .45 smacked Neal in the back of the head. Pat was leading a considerably less verbose Neal up the stairs when Widow appeared in the front doorway. The sight of what he assumed was another cop, this one in his house, reinvigorated Neal's posturing.

"Wow, illegal search. You guys might as well not even take me in," Neal said as they walked onto the porch.

"You need to see this," Widow said, ignoring the babbling man.

"Neal Maxwell," Pat said.

Widow glanced at Neal for half a second. Simultaneously, he yelled down and dove back inside the house. Pat took the hint and ducked behind the brick porch surround. Ever effusive, Neal continued his verbal assault with such vigor that he appeared to take no notice of their evasive movements. While the scumbag was enlightening his audience with an encyclopedic knowledge of the 4th Amendment, the red dot on the side of his face became definitive. When Neal's practically headless body fell, his arms were still gyrating pointedly. His last words were *Arizona nineteen-sixty-six.*

The squeal of car tires gave Pat the all clear.

"Dammit, we missed," Pat seethed as he got up.

Widow stepped into the doorway again and smirked at the angry detective.

"Relax, you're better off than him," Widow said. "Or him," he added gesturing behind his back, into the house.

Pat stopped wiping the blood from his shirt. He stepped over the newly departed Mr. Maxwell and followed Widow into the living room.

Other than an overturned recliner, nothing was out of place. Then Pat heard the groan. He rushed past Widow into the kitchen.

Tied to a table leg with telephone wire, a small man, his wispy hair matted with blood, laid face down. Pat grabbed a butcher's knife and cut the man from the table.

"Jesus," he said.

He would've known the guy was a priest by his clothes but had he not seen him before the meat grinder got ahold of his face, he would've never known it was Father Walter Brown.

"I'd say the priest just found out what happens

when a man of words meets a man of deeds," Widow said.

"Damned fool."

"I gather you know him."

Pat didn't deign to respond. He grabbed a rag, wet it, and wiped Father Brown's battered face.

"He'll live. Let's go," Widow said.

Pat shot Widow an incredulous glare.

"He'll live," Widow repeated. "You want to give him CPR?"

"You're a evil SOB."

"It's still early, Detective."

Pat pursed his lips and glared. He looked down at Father Brown again, left him on the floor, and followed Widow to the car. He called emergency on the way out of the house. At the car, he cursed angrily.

"Are you serious? Get over him."

"I'm not talking about the priest," Pat shouted. "If he'd told me what he knew when he had the chance, he wouldn't be in there all jacked up, Dylan would be in jail, and I wouldn't have had the pleasure of meeting you. So no, fuck the priest."

"What, then?" Widow demanded, driving out of the neighborhood.

Pat's phone ringing halted whatever response he would've given.

"Yeah, what?" he yelled.

Pat listened for a minute and hung up.

"Fucking-A right. Of course it is."

"Who was that?" Widow asked.

"Somebody I owe an apology. You're going the wrong way," Pat said.

"You're wrong, Detective. I know his order," Widow replied.

Pat shook his head. "You psychopaths are all so simple. You *knew* his plans. Why you think he shot that idiot from down the street? He'd obviously already been in the house. But when Father Brown showed up, he couldn't trust that he'd be the last one. So he waits down the street instead. If no one else comes, maybe he snipes Maxwell, maybe he goes to the house and gets creative. Doesn't matter; we showed up. Now his shit is FUBAR."

"And you think that'll stop him," Widow said sarcastically.

"No, asshole," Pat said, turning toward Widow. "What'd you say, 'He's just working his way back through lost cases'? What's *the* loss? If you're him and your grand message is being screwed with, all your plans gone to hell, where you going? You gonna keep clowning around in the minors or you going to the big show?"

Widow sighed and rubbed his forehead. Not because he was deep in thought but because it had just occurred to him that had he not been obscured from Dylan the entire time they were at the house, there would've been *two* headless dead guys on the porch.

Two times, Mr. Jacoby. There won't be a third. I promise you that.

REVELATION AND RETRIBUTION

"He'll pay Ted a visit," Widow said.

"Pay Ted a visit," Pat echoed as Widow executed a U-turn that made even Pat grab the "oh shit" handle.

35

"Why are you still here?"

The question caught Rosie off guard. She was sitting inside Laura's private quarters, and aside from the few times she'd been beckoned to Ted's office—for advice, which she still couldn't get used to; to give information; or just to give Ted an audience while he made Carl squirm— she'd spent most of the day with Laura. No stranger to her husband's intrigue, Laura nevertheless seemed completely unconcerned about the machinations of this particular drama. Their conversations had centered on Rosie and her family, especially her grandmother, whom Laura seemed quite smitten with, further endearing her. Rosie was so immersed that when Laura suddenly brought up the present, the reality of who she was talking to, where she was having the conversation, and most importantly, who they expected to eventually show up, came back with a deafening thud.

"You know you can leave at any time," Laura added, filling the silence.

"After I lost the job at the Dispatch, my mama called and told me to come back home. I believe her exact words were, 'Gurl, git yo' silly ass back hur an' hep me pay down dees bills.' I ran back there, knowing my mother was a heartless bitch and her perverted boyfriend would always be around, drooling over me or worse. I said it would only be for a little while. It wasn't. When Ted gave me a way out of that shithole, I ran right to him, even though he'd been instrumental in creating my circumstance. When that detective offered me a lifeline, after he'd kept me locked up in a room for twelve hours—worse than you would treat a damn animal—I tried to run to him. You know what, Laura? I'm really tired of running."

Laura sat back. She mused quietly over all Rosie had told her. She took a sip of wine and glanced up at the young woman she'd accidentally grown close to.

"You might die. Running for your life isn't the same thing as running *from* your life."

It was Rosie's turn to sit back and digest what she'd heard. It was true. As evidenced by the smattering of news that trickled into their little cocoon, the Angel—or Dylan as she'd started calling him—was coming apart at the seams. His Day of Retribution wasn't going quite as planned. He'd had no intention of harming her during their first meeting. He might feel differently today.

"Something my grandmother used to say— something I didn't understand until this very moment. She would say, 'Chile, I don't cur how many times you shit t'day. You jus' make sho t'night when you bow yo' head to the Good Lord that you done wiped yo' ass.'"

When Rosie finally looked up from her feet, Laura's face was pensive. Slowly the sides of her mouth curled, her eyes brightened, and the smile transformed into a full, hearty laugh. Rosie was confused, on the verge of being angry. She couldn't tell if the laughter was in condescension or agreement.

For an interminably long time, Laura couldn't get control of herself.

"Your grandmother," was all she managed to spit out between giggle fits. Finally, Laura covered her face with a handkerchief. She dabbed her eyes while the chuckles subsided.

"Your grandmother," she started again, "certainly had a way with words. So, you think staying here will get the figurative poop off you?"

"I gave Dylan the name and the platform. He was the killer, but the Angel is my creation. I have to see that story come to a close. On my terms. No more running."

Laura nodded. She crossed and uncrossed her legs several times. She rubbed her hands together hard enough to start a fire.

"Rosie, I won't say I completely understand your reasoning, but like my mother used to tell Daddy, when you can cinch yourself into a girdle, stand up all night in these heels, shake hands, and make small talk with the most repugnant collection of human beings ever assembled—all just to make you look good—when all you really want to do is sit on the couch in your robe with a tub of ice cream on your lap, then you can tell me you like the red dress more than the pink one."

Rosie's smile now matched Laura's, wide and bright, not a hint of condescension.

"What did your father do?"

"Why, Daddy was in politics, of course."

36

As day turned to night—an annoyingly dark night—Ted's mood adjusted in correlation. During the day, he was in the middle of the game: making sure Carl stayed together enough to keep the PD pointed at Widow Drake, putting together a preliminary list of who he wanted and where once he took his rightful place in City Hall, and directing his security forces.

In the less-busy times, he was able to amuse himself with stories of the carnage Dylan was levying on the city. His plan in shambles, random killings of "righteousness" were now the order of the day.

In those moments, Ted would look at Carl and think, *I'll be the most beloved mayor in the history of this city, simply for not being you*, with a look of stoic concern on his face.

He had no intention of keeping his promise to Carl Phillips. Eventually, when the time was right, the world would know the Angel was, in fact, Dylan Jacoby, son of former Mayor Carl Phillips. Carl had too many friends, too many loyal to him. Ted had to let them circle the wagons around their fallen friend, barricade the fort against the interloper. City Hall was merely a step, a superfluous phase, in Ted's grand plan, but he wanted it, and he *would* have it.

Let them get close. Let them cheer loudly and proudly, protest with venom and self-righteous indignation. Then I'll blow all their asses to hell.

Thoughts of his future, all the games to be played and won, had danced in his imagination during the day. But when the dusk fell and Dylan had gone quiet, the present became all consuming.

"Sir, aren't you afraid of Widow Drake?" Luis had asked yesterday in the hours before his unfortunate swan dive.

Ted was annoyed at his manservant's audacity, in that he asked the question unprompted, but forgave him since he'd already decided to send the unaware Luis against Widow.

"Why would I fear Mr. Drake?"

"Because he might kill you, sir," Luis answered in a voice that suggested Ted was obtuse for having to be told.

Ted worked mightily to restrain himself.

"No, Luis," he started, his tone curt. "Mr. Drake does not frighten me. As to your larger question, I don't fear death; I fear losing."

"Are they not the same thing?"

At this point, part of Ted was actively rooting for Widow to at least put Luis in the hospital.

"That, Mr. Ortega, is why you serve me and not the

other way around."

Now bunkered down inside his office, with scores of security both on the grounds and roaming the halls of his palatial estate, a blinking red light on his desk phone declared to Ted that he was about to put that very hypothesis to the ultimate test. He walked to his desk on unsteady feet—the first time he could remember being saddled with that particular affliction—and pushed the button.

"Sir?"

"Yes, go ahead."

"We have a problem. CCTV just went down."

"Fix it, then," Ted replied angrily.

"Yes, sir. We'll get—"

A scuffling sound filled the line. Ted stood rooted at the intercom, his finger poised over the button, eyes riveted on the light.

"God tests the righteous and the wicked. On the wicked He shall rain snares, fire and brimstone, and an horrible tempest," the Angel said, his voice grave and raspy through the speaker. "Ted Allen, retribution is at hand."

Ted turned his head just as Carl, suddenly full of life, rushed to the intercom. Carl picked up the receiver, his eyes wide and bloodshot, his hand clutching a clump of silver hair, as he screamed his son's name into the empty line.

Ted went back to his chair. He swirled, but did not drink, a glass of brandy. He crossed his legs and watched the soon-to-be-former mayor lose his last grip on sanity. A sneer formed on his face. His eyes hardened, and his heart thumped rhythmically inside a chest that no longer heaved in apprehension—a crazed killer at his doorstep, and he calmed himself.

Board games are for children. No real incentive to win. No real loss, no real gain.

Ted now knew for certain he was right, and Luis, in all his cowardice, was not.

"We shall see, Mr. Jacoby. We shall see."

37

As Pat labored behind Widow, he cursed the genetic lottery that had apparently blessed his companion. Widow's graceful nature was not relegated to terrestrial activities. Even though he had two bullet holes in him, the assassin easily outpaced and outclassed the detective during their swim across the large lake that abutted Ted's property. And Pat was convinced, much to his annoyance, that Widow was taking it slow for *his* benefit.

By the time the detective dragged himself from the muddy water and peeled off his wetsuit, Widow had already dispatched three of Ted's mercenary security force. Widow noticed Pat glancing down at the closest fallen man as he approached.

"If you're queasy about it, I suggest you stay here."

Pat cursed under his breath and pulled a silenced pistol. He bent down and took the radio from the merc's jacket.

"Not my first rodeo, numb nuts. Let's get to it."

They left the lakefront and started the trek up the hill to the rear of Ted's house. As they wound through the woods, it became clear the radio was unnecessary. The occasional *thump-thump* of suppressed gunfire from the front of the house told them all they needed to know. They forewent stealth and veered to the paved trail. A few minutes later, they emerged from the foliage.

"Ted will be in his office, center room on the first floor," Widow said.

Pat quietly thanked God there would be no more swims, hills, stairs, or other physical exertion not directly related to his present job, and left Widow.

He crept up to one of the back doors just as a shadow passed against it. He ducked behind the wall while the merc, still on rounds amid the danger, came to the door.

Give you this, Ted, you obviously pay well.

The man took a single step outside, and Pat fired. He shot him in both knees and smashed his face in with the butt of his gun. Pat had to club the big man so many times before he went limp, he thought for a second he'd killed him anyway. Once he was down, Pat dragged the unconscious man from the doorway and stepped into the corridor.

Only a few feet into the house, another man clad in black with a submachine gun draped across his shoulder appeared around the corner. He saw Pat a second after Pat saw him.

"Police. Don't do it," he shouted.

Both men were shooting before the sentence finished. Pat shot first. He walked by the dead mercenary, the barrel of his gun still smoking, pissed at the senselessness of it all.

How many people gotta die tonight?

He continued through the house—down circular corridors and blind corners, with hallways appearing out of nowhere and ultimately leading to the same. Pat spent several minutes backtracking after running into dead ends. He felt like he was walking through a maze, which wasn't far off since Ted had had the interior built to mimic the Labyrinth.

"Assclown."

Pat stopped cold. After his outburst, he realized he didn't hear a thing, not the absence of noise but rather the cessation of it. He stood to the side of the door closest to him. He knelt and tried the handle.

The door exploded. Bits of sharpened wood and scorching metal shards peppered his side.

"Motherfucker," he yelled. "Police. Put the goddamned gun down."

The shotgun cocked again.

"Put that gun down, or I swear to God I will kill you!"

"Detective McConnell?"

Pat stuck the barrel of his gun through the watermelon-sized hole in the door. He followed gingerly with his face. He didn't know the woman holding the shotgun, but the woman next to her was immediately familiar.

"What in God's name are you doing here?" he asked Rosie.

"What are *you* doing in my house?" the other woman asked pointedly.

Pat noticed that while the shotgun had been lowered slightly, she still held it at the ready.

"Lady!"

"He's here for Dylan," Rosie offered.

The woman looked from Pat to Rosie and back to Pat again. She lowered the shotgun completely and stood up.

"I'll take you to my husband."

Before Pat could protest, both women were up and headed toward a door on the other side of the room.

"Goddammit," Pat hissed as he hurried after them.

With Ted's wife in the lead, they found their way to Ted's office without being stymied by inane design proclivities. Raised voices greeted them. Pat pushed the wife out of the way and barged into the office.

Mayor Phillips and his son were arguing. Dylan was covered in blood, grime, and considerably less skin on his face than he'd once had. Carl, comparatively clean, still looked the more haggard of the two. Ted sat impassively, viewing the heated exchange as if he wasn't the subject of it.

"Dylan," Pat shouted as the Angel saw him. "It's over, Dylan. Put it down."

Dylan immediately raised his gun.

Carl stepped in front of Pat. "Patty, stop it."

"Carl, get the fuck outta the way."

"Patty, you get that gun off my son!"

Pat's eyes danced between his two adversaries.

Dylan stayed, while Carl advanced. His hands spread wide, he used his body to shield Dylan.

"Caaarl!"

Carl suddenly leaped to Pat's side. Pat crouched reactively as slugs meant for his head tore into the wall behind him. He returned fire. One of the shots hit Dylan in the leg just as he dove behind the desk.

"McConnell, you self-righteous prick, put that goddamned gun down."

Pat glanced behind him. Ted's wife was laid out. Carl was now in possession of her shotgun and had it pressed into Rosie's chin.

"Carl."

"Shut the hell up, McConnell. You think I'm gonna let you kill my boy over this piece of shit?"

Dylan limped from behind the desk and pointed his gun at Ted.

"This is how this plays; you're gonna drop your gun," the mayor said.

Carl had more to say, but the man who always moved with deadly silent intent now stood behind his son, one gun pointing at Dylan's head and the other in the general direction of Carl. A father's instinct to protect trumped logic and reason. He threw Rosie to the floor so he could get to Widow.

What he achieved was giving Widow a larger target. Three shots went off like a machine gun burst: two center mast and one to his forehead.

Dylan registered his father's death, but he spent his last moment staring into Ted's eyes. He shot and was shot in virtually the same instant. The Angel smirked on his final descent.

When the smoke cleared, Widow stood over Ted while Pat rushed to Rosie, who was trapped under Carl's body.

"Shit. That hurts."

Pat and Rosie looked over as Widow faced Ted. Ted looked exactly as he had all evening, except for the red spot growing larger on his right side. It was obvious, despite his attempt to look otherwise, that he was in extreme pain.

"It won't hurt long," Widow said.

He had the Luger pointed at Ted's face. Pat had started to move in their direction when, without taking his eyes off Ted, Widow shot twice, directly over Pat and Rosie.

"That wasn't a mistake. We've had a productive day together, Detective. Don't make me change my mind."

Pat held Rosie behind him. He glared at his *partner*.

Ted felt suddenly as if he were surrounded by children about to throw tantrums. "Don't be so dramatic, Mr. Drake. You're not going to kill me."

Widow smiled. It was not meant to engender warmth. Ted held up an arm.

"Mr. Drake, give me just a moment. If you're not convinced, kill away."

Widow was bemused.

"Hah. Fine, Ted. I'll play."

"Very well then."

Ted grimaced as he lifted himself from the chair. He stepped over Dylan's body as if it were a throw rug and staggered to his desk. Widow followed closely, one gun on Ted, the other still pointed at Pat and Rosie. Ted fell into the chair and reached beneath his desk.

"Careful," Widow said.

Ted glanced up at Widow and then Pat, rolled his eyes, and produced a small case. He reclined as he was accustomed to doing and in the process pressed his shoulder into the chair back. He groaned and doubled over in pain while Widow checked the contents of the case.

Almost immediately, Widow's demeanor changed.

"As I said, Mr. Drake, don't be so dramatic," Ted said through gritted teeth.

Widow smiled again, this time without fatal intent, and holstered his guns. He closed the attaché case and started out the door he'd come in.

"Wait, wait. Wait a fucking minute. What the hell's going on here?" Pat demanded.

"Good day, Detective."

Widow stepped through the door and was gone. Pat stood in the middle of the carnage, trying to wrap his mind around it all. His gaze traveled over the bodies of Dylan and Carl, the father and son, mayor and former DA, and he shook his head. He then looked back to Rosie, who was helping Ted's wife up.

Finally, he settled on Ted. The man had been shot, he would have to explain at least a dozen dead bodies—paramount among them the mayor of the city—and the master of the game couldn't have looked happier. He watched Pat's consternation with amusement.

"Don't stress yourself, Detective. It's way above your pay grade."

EPILOGUE

Months later...

Every day she came and sat in the same chair, listening to the same beeping, smelling the same disinfectant. After a night shelling out sin one shot at a time, Rebecca spent the day inside the hospital room of a man she barely knew, who she could never have (and wouldn't take even if one day he offered himself to her), reading from a worn book she hadn't opened since she was forced to as a little girl.

He wasn't going to wake up. That's what the doctors kept telling her. Sister Mary Agnes, the nun from his church, said it too. Parishioner after parishioner came to check on and pay their respects to Father Brown, because they also *knew* he was never leaving.

The fixture in the room, with garish makeup and plunging necklines—who they at first regarded with mistrust, then acceptance, and eventually pity— wanted to tell them all it wasn't about him waking up. Sure she wanted *Wally to get the hell outta here*, but that wasn't why she spent every spare moment with the comatose priest, reading the New Testament so much that she could now recall much of the gospels from memory. On those occasions when she was alone with him, she took off the disguise of obligated friend (which fooled only the wearer) and admitted to herself, the unresponsive priest, and God that she loved Wally more than anyone she'd ever known.

She didn't think Wally would *ever* wake up either, but Rebecca was not going to let that man die alone.

This morning, as always, she sat and she read.

"And he answering said, Thou shalt love the Lord thy God with all thy soul, and with all thy strength," she recited, pausing as tears clouded her vision.

"And with all thy mind; and thy neighbor," a quiet voice, barely above a whisper, chimed.

Rebecca gasped. She covered her mouth, her eyes glued to the pages. She wouldn't look up, couldn't look up. Frightened that hope for the miracles in the book she read daily had seeped into her own soul, terrified that fatigue had finally taken its toll on her and the voice was inside her head—what if she did look at him and he was just as he had been?

Father Brown raised his arm. He laid his hand atop hers, caught the tears sprinkling the gospel of Luke, and squeezed her fingers gently.

"As thyself," he finished.

***

"He'll be ready for you in a few minutes."

Pat shot the mayor's assistant a sidelong glance and walked toward the office for the first time since he'd met Carl Phillips there. The woman jumped up and grabbed him by the arm.

"Lady, you probably wanna rethink your next move." Pat didn't look at her as he spoke. His eyes were riveted to the long fingers wrapped around his bicep.

One by one, the fingers unpeeled.

"Good call," he said as he continued to the closed door.

Lou, after thanking the woman and apologizing for his partner's surliness, followed him in.

Gone was the grey Berber carpet, exchanged for a deep red plush complete with a royal blue path leading directly to a hand-carved mahogany desk. The walls had been repainted and adorned with expensive prints. Everything inside the office was meant to convey the wealth and power of the man behind the desk. And in that spot, Ted, looking as dapper as ever, currently entertained a man for whom *dapper* would never be an adjective.

"You can go," Pat said, dismissing Ted's visitor.

The portly, middle aged man with a permanent tan and sweaty glaze stared at the newcomers with an amused look. "Pat McConnell. Lou Maguire," he said as if reading their names from a cost-benefit analysis.

Lou was suddenly very interested in the man. Pat couldn't give a rat's ass.

Cloak and dagger bullshit, he thought.

"Sam, we'll talk later," Ted said.

The man got up from the chair, groaned, grabbed a briefcase, and walked toward the door. With a smile on his face, he nodded to both men as he passed them. Neither reciprocated, and both felt like he was cataloguing every detail about them—that or confirming what he already knew.

"Gentlemen," Ted said as the door closed.

"What's on your mind, Allen?" Pat asked, though he really had no interest in the answer. The message wasn't missed.

Ted glanced at the two men; one he'd summoned, the other had tagged along. After a moment, he smirked and nodded.

"No secrets, I presume?"

"Goddamn right," Pat answered.

"Well, then," Ted said, unmoved. "Pat."

"Detective," Pat corrected.

"Pat, I assume you know why you're here?"

Pat was used to Ted's mind games by now. Much to his annoyance, he was getting good at playing them himself.

"I'm thinking that while you're settling into your new digs, you got this little thought flutterin' 'round in your pretty little head. You're wondering if the other shoe is gonna drop and bust your whole world apart. Don't fret, Ted. It is, and I'm wearing it."

Ted leaned back in his chair. He crossed his legs and scoffed. "That's a shame."

"For you, yeah, I guess it would be. Don't get too

comfortable, Allen. You won't be here long," Pat responded as he turned to leave.

"No, I won't," Ted agreed, wholly aware they had completely different destinations in mind. "You can go," he added needlessly. "But before you do, remember it's better to be my friend. Or if not my friend, then nothing. Trust me, *Detective* McConnell, you don't want to be my enemy."

Pat paused halfway down the blue pathway, with Lou just behind him.

"That street runs both ways, and, Ted, just so we're clear: you are my enemy," he said without regarding the mayor.

"Detective Maguire," Ted said.

Both men stopped cold; neither had expected Ted to acknowledge Lou.

"Yes, Mr. Mayor?" Lou answered.

"Everything I've heard about you suggests that you're a smart man. You could be a valuable asset to *my* city."

"Ooookay. Uh, thank you," Lou responded.

"But, Mr. Maguire, you've chained yourself to an anvil. What do you think happens to you when that anvil gets thrown in the river?"

Pat was roiled. Threaten him, fine. Threaten his loved ones, and amends *would* be made.

Lou saved his friend. Again. He pursed his lips, concentration lines forming across his forehead. He sighed and shook his head. Then he smiled.

"I appreciate your concern, Mr. Mayor, and I gotta

tell ya, you're right about that. I did go and get myself tied to an anvil. But you know, I got a secret weapon."

Both Ted and Pat stared at Lou with confused expressions.

"Fat floats."

When Lou punctuated the joke with a smack on his substantial belly, only one of them laughed.

"I'll be seeing you, Ted," Pat said, a genuine smile on his face.

He closed the door behind him, silencing whatever response he was positive Ted was still orating.

"I didn't think it possible," Lou said once they were in the elevator. "He's even more of a blowhard than you said. What a crock of shit."

Pat gave his rotund partner a good-natured slap on the back and nodded in agreement. As they exited City Hall, a small, tuxedo-clad man held open the adjacent door. Laura Allen walked by as if he wasn't there, though her companion noticed.

"Detective."

"Ms. Williams," Pat responded. "You working for Ted Allen?" he added, no attempt to hide the judgment in his voice.

"I work *with* Laura Allen," Rosie corrected.

"Big difference I'm sure," he said.

"Ha. You have a good day, Detective, and be careful out there."

"Same to you," Pat responded as he turned.

"Hey, Kemosabe," Lou shouted up from the car. "Davis wants to see you."

Pat glanced back at the building and shook his head.

"Nah, Lou, I'm a little tired of the Allen family. Tell the lieutenant he can go fuck himself. I got police work to do."

COMING FALL 2017:
SHADOW OF THE LOST

1235 C.E.

The Andalusian galloped across the field, its body dripping with sweat, muscles taut from exertion. The horse's heart beat ferociously, pushing blood to waiting muscles, yet giving all too little oxygen to the overworked beast. Its tongue, bloated and discolored, hung out of its mouth, listlessly bouncing. Death coming closer with every step, the Andalusian nevertheless pushed on. Its rider demanded it. Certain death chased them, rider and beast, and the beast would not relent while blood still coursed through its veins. The beast would not fail its master, and so the horse continued, encouraged uselessly by the rider and knowing that each gallop brought it closer to life's end.

Sweat had long since soaked through the man's cloak, clinging it to his back. His windblown face, contorted in agony and fear, was streaked with dirt and dried tears. His shoulders, back, and arms ached from days of constant effort. His body screamed in pain, begging him for rest. The bright sun shone above, indifferent and callous, beating down on man and beast, sapping precious life from both.

But Antonio Marcellus dare not stop. Though he could not see his pursuers, he knew they were there, pushing their steeds toward graves of their own, desperate to catch the traitor.

Marcellus continued the punishing pace day and night, through all manner of extreme weather. Still, death's shadow hounded him relentlessly.

The pair now traveled along a narrow path. The high tops of the trees shaded and cooled them while low tree branches on either side tore at their bodies, eagerly claiming tributes of flesh and blood from horse and rider. They reached the apex of the path, and soft, cushioning earth gave way to hard, unflinching rock. Shading trees opened to a cloudless blue sky and radiant sun.

The Andulusian's body could take no more. Powerfully muscled legs and hindquarters, rippling chest and thick neck all seized as one. The horse simply fell over. Marcellus flew through the air, coming to rest on a bed of jagged rocks.

Aching, he forced his body upright, leaving bright red souvenirs on several of the razor sharp points. He gazed at his fallen comrade.

Legs straight out from its body, the horse convulsed, its head jerking spasmodically. Its eyes bulged, and its breath came only in choked gasps, white frothy spittle covering its mouth. Tears falling freely down his chin, Marcellus unsheathed his blade and walked toward the dying animal, meaning to end his dear friend's torment, when mercifully, finally, the beast took its final breath.

Marcellus knelt over his friend. He said a quiet prayer and kissed the beast. He stood and made his way down the hill. More than walking or running, he simply leaned forward and let gravity pull him down the slope.

Blood flowed generously from deep gashes along his back. It pooled inside his shoes, leaving crimson footprints with every step.

He could hear his pursuers in the near distance now, the constant thudding of hooves, a steady rhythm of impending doom, but the sound of rushing water and the relief it promised was what filled his ears. The waters of Italy's Tiber River beckoned him.

He approached the bank of the Tiber and fell to his knees in the cooling water, a circle of brown and red immediately surrounding him as the muck and blood was washed from his body. He cupped his cracked, dry hands and submerged them. Looking down at the reflection, Marcellus saw himself for the first time in days. A grotesque mask of dirt and blood covered all of his face except his mouth and eyes. His lips, dried from days of riding with little water, were swollen and purple. He dipped his head into the river, letting the water wash away the mask, praying that his ride had not been in vain, that the secrets would stay secret.

As he drank, he could hear approaching riders. He didn't have to look, he knew who they were. After one last drink of life-sustaining water, he turned to face his executioners.

The sun shone through overhanging branches, bathing him in warmth and light. The men led their horses to the river, save two who approached him.

"My dear, Antonio," one of them said, sighing as he spoke. "Do not be a fool. Tell us where it is."

Marcellus looked upon the man, tears blurring his vision. "My brother, I weep for you. My heart aches for the blackened deadness that now beats inside you."

"Tell me where it is, and I swear to you we will spare your life."

Marcellus replied by kneeling before them, clasping his hands together in silent prayer.

"God bless you," Marcellus said when he finally spoke aloud.

Both men unsheathed their blades. Marcellus stood, extending his arms upward toward the heavens, a smile on his face.

"Damn you, Antonio," the man said as he drove the wicked dagger down, piercing Marcellus' left breastplate. His compatriot quickly followed suit, driving his blade into the right side of Marcellus' body with such force that his ribs cratered on impact and erupted from his chest, a circle of blood, bone, and tissue.

Blood sprayed from the wounds, covering the faces of the dagger-wielding men. Both blades passed completely through Marcellus' body, their deadly points protruding beneath his shoulder blades. Death came quickly to Marcellus, and his body fell back into the Tiber, his arms still extended toward the heavens, his eyes still on the sun, his face still turned up in a triumphant smile.

ABOUT THE AUTHOR

AK is a lifelong resident of St. Louis. He loves reading, history, his family, and working out— not necessarily in that order. Admittedly, that seems like a pretty boring guy, but wait till you get to know him. Hah!